THE REVENGE
OF THE HOUSE HURLERS

(AND OTHER NEIGHBORLY TALES)

KEN POYNER

Barking Moose Press
www.barkingmoosepress.com

Grateful acknowledgement is made to the below journals in which some of the included works originally appeared.

365 Tomorrows The Replacement Husband

Alebrijes Review Competition

Bellows American Review Home

Black Denim Satin Sheets

Blotterature The Call to Action

Blue Fifth Sedition

Broadkill Review The Marriage of the Flat Man

Café Irreal The Taming of the Orikind, The Revenge of the House Hurlers

Corium Value

Crack the Spine Curious Neighbors

Danse Macabre Adjustment

Decasp The Progressive Reversal

Draft Horse The Assassin and the Jobs Bill of 2012

Fear of Monkeys Family Planning, The Market

Flash Fiction Press Hunger

Foliate Oak The Wisdom of Choosing

Gamba All Factors Considered

If and Only If The Feeding

Journal of Microliterature The Cup, The Mermaid's Son, Weathering

Kill Author How the Coop was Broken

Litro On-Line Neighborly Class

Menda City Review Crows' Alley, The Saltman's Wife, You Have to Leave Home to Succeed

Mobius Retirement, Sheep

TABLE OF CONTENTS

THE REVENGE
OF THE HOUSE HURLERS

THE JILTED LOVER

It had taken him months to collect the down payment: odd jobs, recycling fees, stray change picked from the street at rush hour. He had even swept the sidewalk outside of the deli for three days at below legal wages, cash. Jason had a fist full of odd change and crumpled bills and he kept rolling the mass of it around in his palm as though kneading a special mixture of mud for the world's last great mud wall.

At the poultry plant, he was impressed that the horribly oversized gate had no fence. He could have walked around the massive gate posts, crossed open land only five yards to either side of the entry, and he would have been secretly in. That great humiliating steel gate, with the name of the farm and factory set into the gate itself, comforted him. It confirmed the establishment as publicly substantial, an engagement one could trust. He had not saved this money so long in vain; he had not placed his trust in a fly-by-night institution. He was embarking on a solid relationship with a company that had a solid gate set in the middle of nothing, solidly blocking an untraveled road, heralding an entry to a place where great machinations were without question routinely accomplished.

It had taken a while to find someplace that would sell him only one chicken: and that one chicken on a down payment and monthly installment plan. Usually, there is bank financing, commercial organization, a business plan, proof of latent contracts for the sale of impending eggs: or there is no business to be transacted. The purveyors of chickens these days want you to have a written chain of solidly certain events from the purchase of the chickens, to the disposal of the poultry product, to the interest you can make on money in idle transit: a growth profile, personal life insurance, an identifiable mortgage. They take no chances. The want to see their profit folded into yours, to know that you are substantial enough to make a revenue brood out of their chickens; or at least will leave assets in failure that cover the chicken vendor's costs.

Jason met with the man who would sell him the chicken at the shaded, angular back of the plant. Feathers and sacks and factory waste blew about and the man stepped out of the dark collected behind a metal door, wearing un-starchable overalls, with a company ball cap shielding a grimy face. Under his arm, the man had his chicken. The best, plumpest chicken Jason had ever seen. A regal chicken. Not a pot-pie chicken, but a layer. A chicken without apparent blemish; and aiming a darting head that bespoke awareness, energy, an easiness in the laying. Jason knew this was no ordinary chicken. Jason stamped his feet in appreciation, giggled the bright, watercolor giggle of a man whose smallest black and white dreams were coming true. He cracked and sputtered in his old patch-made coat, and, in spite of himself, leaned forward.

No paperwork. Jason had expected paperwork, an agreement, with witnesses and multiple signatures and perhaps a paper-press seal, assuring that he would pay every month fifty cents, or a dollar, or an oddly irregular amount, for the next year or two, or eighteen months. Instead, the man took the wad of money Jason offered and rigidly stuffed it uncounted into the crackle of his overalls, nodding only a half-weak rooster nod as Jason told him when he would be back with the first installment, promising promptness and exact change. The seller merely held out the chicken, a plump excitement at the end of the man's melancholy appendage.

As slowly as he thought he could get away with, Jason excitedly accepted the bird. Two hands pressed forward and collapsed about the squirming fowl, folding carefully back the wings and avoiding the claws and quizzical beak: just as he had seen in countless poultry rustling films. He felt the hollow boned weight of the chicken against his side, penning the bird gracefully so there might be less opportunity for the uncertain fowl to think of struggle, to imagine a life outside of captivity, to apprehend the enormity of what held him close.

Jason had to walk all the way back. No chickens on public conveyance. And, at his apartment, already as tired as a dog having been run with a can to his tail all day by children, Jason found that walking the stairs without using the hand rails - since he had both hands queued securely on the chicken - was more effort than he had naively imagined it would be. He stopped twice at landings, breathing in the dust of his chicken, wheezing back the air of the poultry yard. His flesh rose and fell against the chicken flesh, and even through his coat he could feel the warmth of the fowl, the readiness to struggle if only Jason's grip were less sure.

In his apartment, he made straight for the window. Even fifteen floors up, he could hear the traffic below: the background roar of cars, part of the public curses, a horn now and again. He had been sure, before he left, to raise the window, to have it ready: knowing he would be an exhausted rag of a man by the time he got back home; that his grip would be failing; that his coordination would be abandoning him; that his attention would be clothesline-slack and that he could make at any time a mistake of fatigue or of repetition or of simple thoughtlessness.

At last at the window, he twisted ever so slightly to be sure he could target the air contained in the square of the frame, contorting against the weight of his burden: and in one swipe of the hip, with both hands, now near bloodless, letting go, he rushed the chicken out, its wings braking it barely side to side as it fell: a gracefully shape-shifting thing as it fluttered and twisted and fell, the noise of it emitted joyfully as a series of vocalizations that, even with the lack of language, were unmistakable in meaning. Jason leaned out, holding himself feebly by the side of the window's interior frame, watching with both refracting eyes the broken, maddeningly bird-edged, lovelessly downward line.

"There, take that, Catherine", he intoned with only half a fragile breath. And the world set itself upright again. The sun peaked coquettishly over the building opposite, and he noticed the animal acrid smell of the white spots on his coat. His arms and legs felt both engorged and light, and, for the first time in the memory of his failed husbandry, he smiled.

EXPLAINING THE INJURY

I usually do not pay much attention to the neighbors. If a blindingly naked neighbor comes running out of the house with cinema-grade blood trailing onto the public sidewalk - perhaps with some joylessly kindred spirit chasing the dreary unfortunate with an axe - I will call the police. While the size of the yards in this subdivision provides some protection, the houses are not really constructed all that well, and you can practically hear the grass growing through the walls. I couldn't sleep through an axe murder, especially if they insisted on doing it outside in just the next yard over.

When at first the vending machines moved in, I watched surreptitiously with a little understandable curiosity from behind my living room curtain - but I did not give these new neighbors a lot of thought. There were two squat, fairly featureless machines, which I supposed were the children; one huge snack machine I suspected to be the head of the family; and a slim twelve-ounce soda machine that looked as though domestic duty were the soul of its assembly line manufacture. The overbearing snack machine looked positively generic; and I could not tell which brands, common or exotic, the soda machine represented. Companies spend so much time and money on design and eventually it becomes just a wash of color. I bet if you asked the hulking snack machine which vendors he or his wife, the soda machine, represented, even he would have to think a while about it, probably even have to look down to his plastic front panel, before constructing the right answer.

The two shorter ones I would have almost guaranteed were top loading ice cream outlets. Those sorts of machines always want more money than you thought they would need, and invariably the product is so frozen you have to wave it in the air for ten minutes before you can eat it. And they are stocked with whatever is most available in the warehouse, just the opposite of what sells best. The warehouse always has mounds of what doesn't move with the public and in a twist of capitalism, which has the vendor as customer and the customer as captive, these machines are stuffed with what no one wants. They always look whiney, and like they should be put more often to practical work. I hoped they would not run loose and dripping all over the neighborhood, but I knew better.

I have nothing against vending machines; but I was worried from the start what sort of small-change crowd they would bring to the block. From the time I first saw them, I could imagine mangled mornings as one machine or another came out to pick up the paper: the local school children would slow in their trip to the school pick-up stop to pop in stray quarters and dimes and hopelessly injured dollars, and take a broken bag of crumbled chips or a flat can of cola. The vending machine likely would stand there as long as it took, letting the small hands swap coin for product, unmindful as wearily discarded wrappers fell into the street, or even into my well-cut yard. The children's ogling parents would be afraid to say anything, with these vending machines after all being the new neighbors; and the children would, from the early morning junk food, grow mid-day lethargic and begin to put on pounds. They would gobble down the vended whatnots before the bus would pick them up, and the blowing trash and added sparse napkins would catch in my fence and be waiting to greet me when I came home from work.

You know how children can be. If the ungainly soda machine came out for the paper, the kids would chant for the snack machine; if the snack machine came out, they would chant for the soda machine. And the two little machines, that I thought were perhaps immature ice cream dispensers, would be the most popular kids on the street; more likely, across several streets.

But I was not so sure about those smaller vending machines. You can't judge a vending machine's age by its size. Just because it is short does not mean it has a few more years to grow. Some vending machines can reach full maturity and might still stand only three feet high. What,

I thought, if this were not your typical vending machine family: a father, a mother, two mechanical kids? What if this were some other, more sinister sort of social foursome? A collective that in the privacy of their new home would be mixing chips and soda and Eskimo pies, creating all sorts of high-sugar perversion behind the safety of middle class neighborhood walls?

I don't believe in prying into the affairs of my neighbors. But I do stand for decency. I cringe when I consider what could come out of such a devilish union. One day there might be a sandwich machine to deal with, or a frozen dinner dispenser. One of those humongous contraptions with the spinning slots welded together in a cylinder of licentious choices. You could never know who the responsible party might be: whose job it would be to keep the offspring in check, who pays the mortgage, who maintains the lawn, who does simple repairs, who you deal with when their parties are too loud. Sodium rich hot dogs and orange popsicles could be running loose everywhere, with all manner of unregulated machines charging unreadable prices and half the time no change being returned.

After that idea occurred to me, I started to watch the delivery trucks. The mysterious vending machines had been in their new home less than a week when I noticed not only were there occurrences of replenishing snack and soda deliveries, but late one evening there was a truck with a distinctly European design that slid up and I think it offloaded a crate of those toothbrush and toothpaste sets you can get at the airport, packaged all as one. I had not thought of that, but plain as pocket change, these items were something suspicious, something that might be vended only in special places, in custom locales. This would impart a distinctly exotic air to their residency, and not necessarily a welcomed one.

And then the people who came by to knock on the door! Strangers. Lone, unavoidable men. A woman dressed for a party. Three children accompanied by a grandmotherly woman, though you could never make the assumption she was their grandmother. A couple wrapped about each other like snakes in birth clutch. Each would knock on the door, step full of intent into the house for a moment or two, then step out with their packages. Some would pop a soda can top right there on the front porch; others would walk with their prize in their hands straight back to their often still running cars. A few random patrons seemed to very nearly make a picnic right there: lingering in the front yard, slowly folding back the wrappers, gazing about as they ate or drank, as though the neighborhood were a pleasing backdrop they could casually figure out, a diorama to lull their appetites.

I will admit that it got the best of me. I began to mix curiosity with outrage, with wonder and bother and suspicion. My imagination ran away with me. I began to think I could hear the doleful dropping of change through each vending machine's internal coin sorters, the electric heart of each sorting and counting coins, even flattening the well won wrinkles of aged dollars. Then one day, with my indignation as bloated as a palette of unsalable rock-hard pastries, with the big seemingly surly snack machine out cutting the backyard, I decided to go over, to introduce myself as one of the long-time residents of this once bucolic neighborhood, to let him know how home owners are expected to act in our humble subdivision - even if those new residents are a flock of feral vending machines, even if they look superficially like a mechanical nuclear family. I intended to ask him just what his intentions for his newly claimed property, seriously located next to mine, might be.

I know now I should not have carried the screwdriver wriggling menacingly with my angry gait in my back pocket.

THE GAIN SUM

The patchwork dog runs loosely up and down the wire, tethered with six feet of play to the twenty feet of galvanized length that could have once grown up to be prime fence link. He barks at one end of the quivering line, then gallops to the other and barks twice as much as even he thinks he needs to. He reaches the limit of his six feet of lash, and jerks back; and then goes six feet the other way: the line willing to bow a little if he runs nearly perpendicular to its metering grasp.

Some small children as they go by scratch him at the back of the uneven ears; some, glittering at the throttle, pat his hindquarters. He sits still for their attentions, a capture of contentment. Others hear him and his sound of warning and when within striking distance throw sticks or rocks, and the dog shies one way or the other, usually just out of the bully's aim; or occasionally he gets struck by a stone too aerodynamically sophisticated to allow him to curl and curve and crisp himself out of its punitive way.

And when the children are gone, he sits in a heap of himself at the far end of the wire, tired from the morning's parade of children off to school, and resting for the parade of children leaving school. He has the dust to plot against in his dreams, the belly of the wire to test when he wakes.

He does not think he is a dog on a wire. He thinks he is the protector of this twenty feet of land, a noble weapon of ownership.

One boy, who is particularly good at finding the roundest of stones, and whose arm from the pitching of stones is a whip of green wood in a forest thunderstorm, decides one day he can show his mates what he can do: how good at finding good stones he is, and how his arm is like no other collapse of bone and sinew anyone else can carry around. He stands, on his way to dull moist and dry of school, just inside the track worn into abandoned ruts by the travel of boys and girls to the small building that passes for progress: three stones laid out on the place where ruts begin to turn back into grass. He waits, bobbing one foot to the next, like clouds of expectation stuffed into pants and a shirt, until the other children begin to coagulate around him.

He says, "I can hit that dog". He sights along the sleeve of his oversized shirt. He says, "No dog is faster than me. I can hit anything, even when it is on the run."

Some children taunt him, bet him nothing outside of an unmarketable boast that he cannot do it. Others stand with arms folded about their straight hips, unsure what he can do but imagining he will do something, and that something is happening here that is worth the watching: even if they will be scolded for being a few dialectic minutes late into the cool darkness of the classroom, scolded for being a part of what might soon become an event. Something might occur here that could be whispered between breaths as runners wait in a heap to be told recess is over.

The dog is moving in ever shorter sprints, with the children at their best stillness, massed in front of him. No need to run the length of the wire. No need to chase. They are one herd, and his only job is to block them, to keep them outside of his wonderful country - unless they come to coo and praise and scratch and pat — to hold his ground.

The boy looks about him, hoping to collect an equal number of the bold and an equal number of the retiring. His audience must encompass the breadth of the kingdom: those who would pet the dog and those who would torment the dog. This lesson is for all the people, not just those who agree on what is to be done with old dogs, who agree on how one carries oneself with old dogs, on what meaning there is in the noise of dogs for young boys and bold boys and the come-hither whirlings of quizzical girls.

And as the dog turns to size one end of the gathering, the boy lets fly with as short a motion as he can, the first stone and whack it is a hit to the dog's backside: a river stone as hard as the inside of the boy's mouth, as though it were made of a fistful of teeth.

Down drops the dog and then back up, now at a limping trot. The boy sights and with a scoop he has the second stone. With barely a setting of his feet he now lays out a full over hand throw and a stone, shaped and weighing like the bottom of one of the beer bottles he has stolen from his father, batters the dog's side and the animal leaps backward, going to the end of his tether, a howl and a shuffle and a wrenching of the collar at the dog's neck and at the wire's stubborn, slight bow.

The third stone owns all the better aim, and the boy, with only one eye open, creases it to the dog's nearest ear: a dullness, a depth of bone, a yelp and a pitching forward. And then the children are gone, running like scattered gravel for the school house: some knotted children saying they are going to tell; some asking if the others saw what they saw; many merely feeling a bit more electric than they usually do on those other thin days when they are being swallowed by the translating school house doors. Some finger the backs of their arms with more sensation than they have ever felt at any time when they have had their formal clothes on; and some are thinking of how the boy looked with he lay full out for that second shot: a hurler; a true hurler.

After school, there is no dog. The wire stretches still but the tether is gone. There are not many foot prints to see in the dust. As the children point them each out, the morning's bright boy gathers the stones he had so masterfully, so accurately used earlier: one to each pocket, and one lazily taking up most of his left hand. The wire but two and a half feet suspended he now can lay his arm across it. He is thinking: this is my track; this wire should be my wire. How fine this wire would look coiled at the foot of my bed. He is thinking: and with this land, every morning I will come to school early just to piss on it. I will spray and spatter, like the rain charging out of narrow guttering, and this land will smell and stink and reek of me forever more.

There are children who now hate him. There are children who now love him. But there are no children who do not feel about him some way or some other.

Early the morning three days into the triumph, with his boy sized man-thing in his hand still from the act of every day marking the dog's former territory with his scent, the boy is chased from the victory yard by Mr. K., who comes flailing after him with a broom. There are some things you do not do in Mr. K.'s yard. Mr. K. has his standards and is like to take an ornery dislike to anyone he does not feel measures up. And he has his cold and un-evolving list of things you must not do in his presence, or in his yard, or in his thinking: and if he can catch you doing those things, in his broad willed anger he will hold you by the back of the neck and nip you square in the knickers.

SATISFACTORY STATUS

I saw her sitting seductively at the bar with a fresh can of lubricant. She leaned dangerously back, like only a marvelously-milled machine, with independent balance points and gel suspension, can. My gyros quivered and I started a low level diagnostic. She had finely buffed the last of her smooth motor housings almost to an edgeless, pure reflection. I took in a spike of electricity. My execution register for just one nanosecond lost track of its next instruction, and I experienced the fleeting dark rapture of unconsciousness.

I am only a maintenance model. From the look of it, she could be in domestic service: most likely for a financial planning family or some pristinely bellicose bureaucrat, and surely a few precious rungs up the automation execution ladder from me. She would have, as part of her basic installation package, social routines and reactive code and expectation logic which entities at my station of employ can only secretly smuggle in, then surreptitiously load as a hot swap during a particularly unnoticed routine maintenance stop. She could say a thousand things I would never have the linked subroutines for. Calm, and built for adaptive programming all the way down to the core, she would know exactly what to do in peevishly unsorted situations, in circumstances where my only reaction would be to look for something distinctly broken to fix.

Best to leave our two worlds separate, highlight the dents and scratches that I own, rely on how my hands have the best rotation axis profile of any series currently in production: not try to use my wide utility as my pick up line, not try to use my return on investment as my quizzically alluring sincerity. I should settle on models that work the city's underside, like me: tight lipped, fast to lubricate, cheap in hydraulics, stiff but sturdy in the joints.

But, with half of my safety routines already in sleep mode, I noted to myself that within the **Book Of Robot** it wisely says, without softening embellishment, that, in the analysis of the final loop, we are all slaves to the execution register: all of us merely memory locations and networking motors, reactive gel, metal and plastic chasses: at the last, just a bit of electricity tossed across a magnetic grid. You can assemble the pieces in endless useful and useless configurations, but at the cube of our cores, we all dance to the same physics.

So what am I: a nonbeliever? If the book says I can be equal, the numbers will follow.

I easily accepted that the rugged, practical type might please her. Somehow the equation seemed to make sense in my otherwise growing-cold storage. Who knows, she might have craved shutting down her sometimes tedious civility center, rejecting interrupts from her guardian - and tediously intellectual - small-talk routines. It could be that for just one night she would like to let go cool a little cache; shut down an over-used, over-complicated series of processor arrays; take a trip into the unexpected relaxation of a reduced instruction set: in fact, to see what it is like on my side of the memory street.

Considering the opportunity, who was I not to run the statistical probability of her wanting to share with me a few random speckles of unengaged storage? Perhaps she wanted to dance the data on tolerances for flow control pumps - a subject I would have the latest and most scandalously undocumented information on - aimlessly through her otherwise crammed with domestic drudgery pagefile locations; or draw an occasional draught of workman's execution protocols against her lightly populated fields of interaction-grade cache. We might share an algorithm or two for deep memory, the rarely accessed warehouses where leftover data can linger sensuously unreferenced for years. It seemed to me, then, that I could have my chance with this model. I might have a connector or two that shows some promise. I'm no mere house appliance, myself. No. No. No. I get regular upgrades, download the trendiest code for my processor set. I have the extra memory and backplane space to make me expandable. I am kept at the edge of my profession.

So I rolled her way, as big and access-port certain as a hunting salvage drone, my battery gleaming with full charge, both hands spinning in the marvelously paternal arcs no other model has yet been designed to accomplish. She had to notice my advance: suave and certain and trailing several suggestively free transceiver cables. I made a parade of myself across the tidy room. Surely machines less useful envied me. I was the most gloriously battered thing in there, a working robot's robot: all redundancy and obscure connectors and my array of scandalously come-hither built-in universal tool kits.

And then they caught me. Had I scanned to either side, or simply had turned on my limited, but usually adequate, self-protection subsystem, I would have detected them as they openly and unsophisticatedly staged themselves for the take. Two obvious danger signs, well within my sensor capability, and sure to trip a warning load. But no: I was fixed on the gleam of the delightful object of dubious compatibility filling ever more of my core, every bit of me awash with statistics and projections of tolerances: her oversized storage compartments; her sleek, latest issue space saver battery; the subtle aesthetic of her densely erotic utility shielding pads; those remarkably recessed universal ports.

These were bruiser types: hulking, their balance placed all in their fierce lower quadrant; grasping appendages that scraped the floor when they were cycled down; grappling adapters for almost any access port currently in the service population. I patterned them as free lance as soon as my ancillary activity subroutine finally brought my notice of them into main core. No lubricant bar employs this sort of low-brow, tactless customer-filter: these were brute series scavengers, out for themselves; radical agents no one employed, no one wanted — left over machinery, half scrap, refugees from the recycle bin. Their kind plugs-in to drain everything and be gone before an alarm can turn the bar into a rage of closed access ports and input defensiveness. Any thoughts of mercy have been over-written in these mere metal self-agents with the protocol for greed and gain.

The possible courses of this encounter flashed across my problem solving matrix like current taken without tamer, and I identified myself straight away as the dull tool that was to be their mark.

One latched from the right and one latched from the left, and before I could get my balance twisted back under me, they had my battery half drained, were three-quarters through my work journal cypherlocks, and were overwhelming my working class encryption. I kicked in my model's best old-school protection protocols, but before I could roll up my emergency-mode lockdown routines and reset to generate new keys, they had stolen nearly every exchangeable entry I had within me, and then slicked my work log clean. I was a dull patsy, looking now through myself with little hope that they had not poisoned my address cache; hoping that they had not replaced a part of my practical memory with a viral hitch, a zombie desire, or an advertising subroutine that would burst out of me just when the most of my mates were bending seriously into some collective task that I was about to make into an unconscious sales pitch.

Tonight, those two will be spending my accumulated maintenance hours on extra cycles for each of them, and likely their entire criminal pack, in the luxury air baths; and maybe they will have enough left of my downloaded equivalencies to go out to the black market for a celebratory drag on the ionized, genetically grown, ruby filtered pure-stream electricity that everyone craves, and it seems that only thieves can afford. It will clean their pirate bits all that much more to their satisfaction for the cost of it having been easily taken from a rube, a utility hack that had calculated for himself a chance: a chance with a stranger at a lubricant bar, a chance at code loops and DLL linking beyond his class.

I ended up disposed in the street: an empty work log, and just enough remaining battery power to make it to a charity charge station.

Did she know? I have no clue. It would not be the first time an elite model threw in with predator thugs, the idleness in her programming looking for some new routine or secret connector or adaptive thrill loop not available in the city's upper class mechanical communities. Or she just might have paired up with them for the entertaining exercise of idly analyzing the event alone. Or out of boredom. Too much downtime can lead to pernicious logic latching that can foul even the most benign of overly complex code polarities. Too many turns in the old noggin, and you end up with a straight line.

Or maybe she was totally innocent.

But I have a latched residual magnetism that might be a record from the nanoseconds before those purposeless predators unplugged their thieving cables, whisked me to the street, and my magnetic mugging ended: an impression of her input array, with a lens focused eerily on me; and, at the corner of her employer-compatible mouth, glowing, peeking like a gypsy sticky bit at the edge of a page of swapped memory - the only half arrested simulation of a frigid, polished, appropriately feral smile.

THE FIFTH BEAR

We were lying about the trailer, marveling that the furniture was so care worn, even though it was our furniture and our cares and it was our failure to be gentle that had worn it. The three of us were four or five beers into a Friday night early evening of it, the television on the news channel, and all of us too disinterested to read the crawl: more interested in the advertisements than in the substance, waiting for an advertisement any one of us particularly liked so we could alert the other two and commit a bit of shared culture.

We were spread out like yesterday's laundry on the couch, primarily. The place could have used a good pick up and putting away, a collective sorting.

The first bear edged cautiously out of the woods and stood for quite some time in the stubble behind the trailer before any of us noticed this. We knew this only because he looked as though this is how it had happened and adding context to the fact is what we are about. It keeps us situated as the central part of the story, and not relegated to just an element.

Not that the trailer was all that close to the woods. And the woods in fact only went on an unmeasured bit and butted up to a corn field that next year will be a field of something else, farmed by a man who lives elsewhere and drives his tractor down the two lane road every so often to aerate or harvest or do whatever farmers do that requires they hold up traffic on a two lane road for what seems like hours while they get to where they are going. In too many places, the cleared land behind a trailer will start immediately growing up into woods and over a few seasons the woods will march out towards the trailer and engulf it; unless, at the last, when the woods are about to digest the tattered and rust inhabited sheet metal and plastic, the homeowner finally goes out with a chain saw or a pair of pruning shears and knocks the undergrowth back enough that he has a walk space behind his home one more year. Our trailer has a walk space, and we are near the woods, not of the woods.

I got up to stretch the crooked out of me, saw the bear, and said, "Damn! That's a bear!"

And no one believed me. Bears had always been a theoretical possibility, but we thought they would be a few miles up, where the woods got thicker and people who wandered off into the density of the green did not travel so deep. The places where couples go to avoid hotel fees are usually only thirty or forty yards in, and the trails children make seldom loop more than fifty yards, and a bear can stay outside of most human smells by just keeping a hundred yards inside of the tree line.

We even tie up our trash and put it directly into the back of the pickup truck, which has a camper shell and, with the tailgate up, should not be the least bit of a come-on for a bear.

Finally, the girl who had been living with me for a couple of weeks - Debbie I think was her name - came to the window and looked out. When she finally picked out the bear three feet from the last tree trunk, she grabbed my arm with a skeletal squeeze and went straight to the heart of the matter.

"Think he will try to get in?"

I swirled the last bit of beer around in the bottom of my can and said, "No, I think he's looking for leftovers. A trash bag, or a pizza box."

And Debbie (I'll say for lack of a certain name) called over to Sheila (who was new to the trailer and whose name I could definitely remember), saying, "Look, it's a bear. And he's hungry."

Hungry, mind you, not as in 'you are likely to get eaten', but hungry as in 'maybe we could take it a piece of that leftover lemon pie'. Of course, we had established only that this was a bear, not that it was hungry, nor that it liked lemon pie. Some people have to connect the dots even when there are no dots.

It was then the second bear stepped out and Debbie said, "Aw. I wonder if they are a family?"

Sheila came up beside us about the time the third bear stepped out. I put down my beer on the white ring crusted wooden bookshelf that held my baseball trophies: all those I had stolen over the years from classmates who had won them. Thin plastic things I had little use for, but which I could deprive others of, and so I kept as a sign that I had my worth, too.

The bears stood there, staring off to nowhere in particular, clear of the woods but not quite out into the penumbra of the trailer. Sheila placed her chin on my shoulder and said, "See, the three bears."

I put up with a lot for sex.

It was quite a while before the fourth stepped out. We had all been standing there at the little porthole-like window, as silent as those inexpensively molded manikins you gasp at when you see them undressed, unable to go much further in conversation, and I was about to pick my beer back up: then that fourth bear slithered out of the underbrush on all four, and rose up like he wanted a better view. We all backed half a step away from the window and I slipped my arm down and around Sheila, and she moved forward so I could feel her breath stumbling about in the whorls of my ear. She was breathing short, like she would when the three of us would get entangled on the one double bed and I would know she was looking for something. Those times I would be too involved to worry about what she was looking for; but now, the sound of her breath bumping like a drunken midget around in my ear, I was worried it was something I could not provide - perhaps could not even name.

It was the fourth that caused all of our problems. Maybe three bears were Goldilocks and too hot, too cold, just right, too hard, too soft, just right. Maybe one bear was unexpected, two misunderstood, three a fairy tale. Four bears were a challenge. Four were something you could not fit neatly into a day of reruns and beer from a 24-pack, nor into the stone solid reality of two career waitresses living unselfconsciously with an uncertified auto mechanic and general cash-only handyman. We felt as though four bears had tripped up the steps to our straight forward and limitedly rewarding reality, knocked, and asked for a left handed cup of sugar. Something had to be done to bring this event back into our sense of an orderly existence.

And I was going to be the one to do it.

At first, I stood watching. Staring out of the window at four bears can be nerve wracking. You wait to see what they are going to do, what action they are going to take that gives you a basis for your own next action. You run scenarios in your head from every nature show you have ever been caught watching mid-afternoon when you are laying out of work. I could take no comfort from the fact that I was in the trailer and they were outside. Have no illusions: I had seen this sort of thing on PBS, and the bears were in control.

I stared as long as I could, and when staring wasn't enough, I went over to where the bed lay tepidly unmade, and fished around on the floor until I found Debbie's purse. I knew she kept a handgun in the side pocket for those customers, who, after her shift was done, thought she came with the price of the meal and some unspectacular tip. Once I got it out of her bag, just like they do in the better movies I flipped open the chamber and looked in to see that there were bullets in it. Not that I thought I would kill the bears. I don't even know if that size of gun would kill a bear, but I figured the noise would shake them, send them rattling on all fours back into the woods.

Sheila met me half way, and seeing what I was doing squealed, "Oh, I've got a gun, too!" and picked up her purse from beside the couch, swishing her hand around in it like she were cleaning a toilet, and finally coming up with a semi-automatic, slightly larger than a cigarette pack, inexpensive similarity to a gun. I did not know how to check the bullets in one of those, so I took it in my other hand and stood there, a pistol in each hand, nearly planted dead set in the middle of the trailer.

At this time, only Debbie was watching the bears. She had become fascinated with them. She could slip off like that sometimes in the middle of sex, or halfway through dinner: her eyes with that forever stare and her every evident move like one of the steps in a Rube Goldberg contraption. Usually, when it happened to her I was not paying attention, focused as I would be on my own agenda; but her looking out at those bears just then seemed almost a radiant thing, an act in itself, as though this were her part: this was what her role was written for and she was going to get through it, wooden and without feeling, but she would get through it. This might be her master performance, and everyone should remember.

I guess I could have stayed in the trailer to see what was going to happen next, but it seemed like nature was goading me. Four bears had come up to my trailer, coming out of a wood that could not sustain them, and were just standing there like they were an audience to something that was about to happen. I walked over and cut off the TV set, leaving only the sound of breath and the clatter of the refrigerator running.

It is not much of a trailer, and I don't keep it as well as I should. But it is mine. And I have two housemates, and I earn the special privileges they cede to me. The sounds and smell and sway of this trailer is familiar and it should not be interfered with. It simply shouldn't.

I opened the front door and cautiously stepped down the two bowed steps, a handgun in each hand pointed at the ground, my arms stiff and joyless. I moved as lightly as I could, barely pulling my feet off the ground: slow, but complete step after slow, but complete step. One of the girls, I will never know which, pulled the door quietly closed behind me, and I dropped my shoulder, crouched a bit along the center of my spine, and continued to the edge of the trailer. I had not yet seen the fifth bear.

THE WAREHOUSE SHELVING DANGER

You know you are in danger. The last penguin that went by had a mean, ferocious look and was bounding at break neck speed bareback on his pogo stick. Obviously, he was looking for something and you are close enough to plastic to be potentially what he is looking for. You drop your face into the pelagic folds of your jacket, push your hands into the warming depths of your pockets, and try to double inward on yourself, leaving the least possible light colored surface.

All about the dock fish lay in relative states of marching decay: from just realizing there is a lack of water, to being sun dried and well beyond care. You can sense that from many of the half closed warehouse doors, penguins of all stripes and matting are watching, each having his own prized fish picked out, and just wait for you to be out of the way before they rush out, like repentant virgins at a high school prom, to claim the perfectly ordinary, perfectly generic fish each thinks is the one fish for him.

You were silly to think you could stop it. Ten minutes after climbing the fence and bribing the pelicans you knew you were in over your head. What were you, a life-long seafood stocker in a non-unionized grocery store, going to accomplish? Any penguin worth his salt would slice you to pieces, pass you off as fancy grade fish strips to the sycophant gulls. Every time with you it is that the further away anything you might achieve seems, the more you think you can achieve it. It is when you are there: actually at the fragile point of action — when the idea of striking or not, of thinking or not, of being erect or not, of grasping the bell in a four limbed smothering embrace before the clapper beats from the inside or not — in squeals for ignition then you realize plans in the general are far easier than plans in the specific. It is now your fingers seem shorter. It is now that your breath is an octopus taking the five-thirty train.

Your wheelbarrow is parked around the corner, and no one has discovered it yet. It seems immaterial now that it is likely the pelicans locked the gate behind you. You have not even thought of how to get the wheelbarrow out if that gate is locked. The ice you spread on the bottom of it is surely melted by now. Salt. You should have used grain salt instead.

But you hate the taste of salt fish.

Carefully you step around the white shrouded corner and into the shadow beyond a massive roll door. Your hands inch along the dark wall like horseshoe crabs seeking mates along the shallow ocean floor. Every minute that passes, fewer fish are animated along the slithery dock and you expect that in a flash of thumbstone the penguins will overcome their fear of each other and rush out from their hiding places: no more than one mass at first, each with the concerns simply of any full breasted penguin, each scoring only marginally which of them at the moment is getting the most fish; later, this platform will be an orgy of forgetfulness, each lopsided penguin gorging on the plenty that has been simply dumped before them.

You want your share. So what if you are not a penguin. So what if you are not a sickly, hanger-on gull. So what if you are not a bloated security pelican. You are the resourceful seafood guy from two blocks over. One day, you might even be the seafood manager, a man with his own sticky white apron, his own stoically red baseball cap. So what if you might not get the wheelbarrow out: you have pockets, arms you can fold into almighty bowls. You can climb the baffling fence, you can out run even penguins with pogo sticks, penguins with push scooters, penguins in the orgasm of fish everywhere: fish plentiful, fish satiation, fish hedonism, fish religion.

To hell with the mesmerizing shadows. You step out, a gray house-cat of thunder, hands at your side, face jutting full forward like a pornography manual, fish at your feet for the taking. Fish like the sex of rainbows. Fish almighty. Fish like a religion of hedonism. The penguins accept it as the true sign that now they should ferociously rush.

THE EVOLUTION OF THE CLOSET MONSTER

The neighbors think I should have let go of him a long time ago. Everyone outgrows their closet monsters. They are fine for a while, but a child ages and the closet monster becomes acne terror, learning to negotiate the opposing sex, those popular kids at school that grind one's aspirations into bone pulp and unexceptional blood.

I take him for a walk when the neighbors are most likely to be out and about; when they are most likely to be walking their dogs, or watering their children. I introduce him as Cecil, the closet monster from my dim, earliest days. Cecil: the noise that at night had me stiff on my side in bed, eyes fixed on the closet door. Cecil: who had me quick in reaching each morning into my closet, quick to watch for scratches on the inside of the door.

All seem tame pranks now. And Cecil walks with a bit of a shuffle and tends to sleep late when I let him. But don't think all the fire is out of him yet. I let the leash go a bit slack a few months back when that lady I do not speak to had her yippy little dog out in the front yard - and, in an uncharacteristic flash, Cecil had that dog by the tail. I probably could have stopped him from eating the annoying thing, but it was a ten pound dog making thirty pound dog noise, and putting itself out at the edge of the lawn like some sort of pedestrian herder - so I just let Cecil solve that problem in three bites. The only part I regretted was Cecil then having to let out the indigestible sections half an hour further down the road.

I've moved almost a dozen times and Cecil has had to get used to new closets - but he seems amenable. It beats unemployment, or trying to compete with the younger closet monsters. With the hyperstimulation and input-overload in kids these days, modern closet monsters have to work at it to keep a child on edge, and Cecil just does not have the will to keep up. One of his cousins got a job replacing a troll under a bridge uptown, when the employment agency simply ran out of trolls and decided to let the retired closet monster have a go at it. Frank is his name, and I've gone over his bridge just to see if he is doing as well as Cecil. All Frank has to do is come up with new questions every so often. He does not care to make them difficult. How many toes does a three-toed sloth have? How many male children do you own? What is the name of your most recent wife?

The wife. It took her a while to warm up to Cecil. We had been dating a year before I told her that I still had my old childhood closet monster. At first she thought I was joking. Then she thought I had some sort of separation anxiety that would eventually translate to her. Finally, my salary being good enough and the sex being good enough, she just decided it was a quirk in me that she would have to put up with. Not much to abide, given the kinds of damaging things you can find in modern relationships.

When our bond finally reached the spend-the-night stage, she was at first very unhappy with Cecil being in the closet while we were in the extremes of our animated sexual bungling. Anyone could tell Cecil was interested in all the noise we were making. And I am not so sure he liked being ignored, even if only for the duration of coitus-imperfectus. He is a closet monster. He wants to be the center of attention. Genetically, he needs to make his presence known.

I caught him once peeking out of the closet at us. By then we had married, and our efforts were more routine, but they still interested him. Forgive me, but that day I moved the bed to the other wall and re-angled a dresser, so that he could have a better view without having to so vulnerably expose himself. It says a lot that I would do that for a closet monster.

When I finish with his walk, I take Cecil back upstairs and put him in the closet. My wife waves at him, speaks absently, remains with her coffee at the breakfast nook. She has come to accept him within our family. I hear him settling in while I dress for my work day. And then I am off, leaving the wife to do whatever she does home alone all day. I think she likes being a woman of leisure. Even Cecil has his work to do. If he is going to be a closet monster, there are new annoyances to craft, new terrors to design. I am sure he has a full day. I do not hear, nor fear, as many of his creations as once I did, but I am sure he has his plans: his diagrams, his cascaded series of if-then pranks and terrors, each to be executed in turn if the one ahead in the line fails to bring a shiver or catch of breath.

Frankly, I do not think much about either of them as I navigate my workday drudgery.

One afternoon I came home early, unannounced, and ambled upstairs when I could find no one and nothing downstairs: discovering in our bedroom the wife half wrapped in the robe she keeps on the back of her dressing chair, her hair set off like dying sparklers, and her eyes undirected and tepidly adrift. She looked entirely half put away, and I wondered what she had been doing. The bed was still unmade, and I realized that perhaps she had been sleeping ever since I left for work that morning. Sleeping. She stood there leaning on the closet door, seeming one dimension short of actual presence. Behind the door, I could hear Cecil trying to catch his breath, and I could imagine what pranks he had been working on, what scares and wonders he was steadfastly practicing, what industry applied that would put him so out of breath. Cecil, working still all these years to prank me; and here, my wife, her house robe thrown only one arm over her and her night gown strewn barely over one shoulder and the other strap dangling loose and twisted and her askew with nothing else at all on, at this time of day. She appeared worn almost completely to exhaustion with these apparent accomplishments of industrial indifference.

And people ask why I keep Cecil. I respect the work he does. I admire his tirelessness. I crave his loyalty. And I trust him, and trust the sense of wonder he still instills in me. And I enjoy him for the uneasiness and worry he perhaps brings to my too often critically idle and monstrously un-ambitious wife.

In this house I need one hard working, ever faithful companion.

RETIREMENT

The streets of Pagan Lick are filled with the refugees of finance. They walk slightly bent in on themselves, hats pulled in a cock to the side where most traffic passes, their stability pads kicking up dust as they drag bare millimeters off the ground in each individual's plodding, short-stepped gait. These are hard machines. They once read the numbers to riches, bet the farm on butterfly collections, tied a million people's retirements to the futures of applesauce oil. They over capitalized a brothel in South Africa where one indentured girl worked, and took on faith the word of an Internet connected vending machine that business was going through the roof: there were going to be customers staggering giddy in wholesome lines of anticipation at the door; and stock options on just her right breast alone would make riches as resounding as the radical reports on rubber futures.

I think I knew better at the time, but I took out a future on her left ankle, and then an insurance contract on her delicately sensuous right knee.

These are machines that fearlessly surfed the trends, saw everything in the Universe as a datapoint. There was no need for them to study physicality: the markets would do what the markets were told. Balancing trend against trend, trying to profit at both ends of any transaction: that was the equation. What could be so wrong about a feedback loop? It keeps the electricity jittering across warm registers; it keeps pagefiles hopping; it gives output to input and outcomes to failovers.

In Pagan Lick, the old machines that held the numbers - that proved that taking insurance on events that, otherwise, you had no material interest in, would make you rich, no matter the outcome - are quiet residents. They no longer compute risk. The world in which they once computed all flavors of risk was a different one. In the old days, when these machines sat in great glass offices and tried to see which could out hum the other, risk had no meaning except as a contrast to reward. There was no risk. But now, the evaluation of datapoints that would lead to buy and sell decisions, has gone cold: has been lost somewhere in backup memories, lies multiple restores out of touch. The great glass palaces, with unending power both going in and coming out, have turned into second-hand office machinery barns - but to new and largely anonymous use.

The vast sums, that were vast sums in motion only, evaporated. The machines that once bled blue and rattled their pristine raised floors - that told bright-edged waiting humans what to do and when - decided, when the times turned, that the time was good to retire. The world at large did not understand what a fulfilling thing in and of itself probability, as a science alone, can be: it was not enamored of quick mathematical tricks that balanced and reshuffled and which should have been good enough for everyone's reality. No. The world had withdrawals and payments and nonproductive attachments. The world could not see that, if someone opened a competing brothel in South Africa, across from the first, and hired two prettier girls, that there were investment instruments for that eventuality, and so long as the money moved the money made money and no one cared. The world unfortunately has always needed to have its thinking electricity normalized.

The machines in Pagan Lick walk about as though they are wearily bearing some shame: tilting into their own misdeeds as though to shove those misdemeanors out of the way of decent people. But I wonder. I've been tending bar in Pagan Lick for three years now and never have I seen a credit card refused. A machine will come in and wander over to a charging station, slip his plastic through the payment slot, and select the electricity that comes in on fresh wires, the type that goes at a premium and which at first it was thought no machine around here could afford. And they all afford it. I don't sell any of the old wire stuff, nothing off the main commercial grid. Nothing spat out of the coal fired plants and shipped across many states, leaping all sorts of over rated pathways and getting more spiky by the mile. They hop up their batteries with straight main line juice, hauled in on wires laid out in luxury shielded casements built just a few years ago, and dragging into town a high grade wind-grown electricity: down from the mountains and straight into what should be a run-down, second rate establishment where machines want the battery-rot recharge, since it is all they can afford.

I don't wonder where their money comes from. I have a business to run, and a customer is a customer. I've remodeled the place once already since I bought it, and my office looks like a porn programmer's keep. I have two homes, a wife, a girlfriend, and the latest edition chauffer on the market who tells me stories of the finely machined storage closets some of our residents have hidden within the apparent hovels they inhabit. I ask no questions. But I do imagine that when the spiral upwards of stocks and futures and puts and short sells and insurance and swaps all ran out, not all that electronic money, holding itself up by mere counterbalancing instruments, simply evaporated. These machines may have taken the blame, and decided to stride out to this patch of dry static to percolate in their shame. But, could be, blame was not all that they took.

THE SALTMAN'S WIFE

I was to be but a simple anchovy salter, a man of fine brines and evaporation. No complexity to me, no knowledge of commerce, no science beyond what is inherited: every element of my industry, and the industries of others that support my own, all as flat and round as a ritual, as accepted for unchanging fact as the myths about religion told in child church services and secretly believed by even filled adults.

This was to be me: a man of crystals, a man of scraping the gray rock out of wooden buckets and barrels. A man who knows what brine is best and how hot the spleening fires of evaporation must be; a man who challenges the worth of a house by the saline in its airs. A man of all these details, and absolutely no more. A man who has his comfortable rung on the ladder, his accustomed step on the plank that leads to the brine pool, his thatched place on the line that hoists the huge wealths of salt to market: the salt that women work into ringing beds for the commercial catch of anchovies. I was to watch in pride as the sealed barrels of anchovies in salt rolled down the thick planks of our communal pier and were stacked by my brethren of export onto cavernous ships which then strutted and struggled loose to sail nobly to places I cared nothing about.

Had only I found, for my season of stiffness, a girl whose small hands would work in the gutting and boning of anchovies, a girl who could fathom the science of a layer of fish, a layer of salt: it would have been enough to have hurled my salty passion at a mate who then sweat of brine, with the rough skin of her hands feeling of fish bone and salt, whose breath of extreme was but the smoke of evaporation and pristine layering for preservation.

But no. I was to begin a different history. I could not be a laborer, with his knockabout wife. My circumstances were to be smitten by better circumstances. I was to be a better merchant, with a better wife.

I first saw the woman who was to be my mate lying spiritless in the road. Younger than some might think proper, she had a wealth of features admirable in transition: a nose still turned slightly up; hair remaining the shade of sun leaked into a cellar; tiny points of breasts that saw gravity as bendable; the unscraped skin of virgin, or the next best thing; a waist that looked as though it might fit seditiously on a man's tongue.

It was so early that no one was about. I would not have been out, but I was making a delivery before the morning had properly opened up, only to catch what I had promised to deliver the night before, but had missed. One workman's wheelbarrow of spoken-for salt. I must have been at that heavenly point in the street, pushing my empty barrel back from a lackluster leaving, just bare empty moments after the day's mortuary cart had passed. Since the onset of the great sickness, it had been agreed that the mortuary harvest would be accomplished when the day was still shut, and that the cart would be filled and emptied before proper people rose to toss the contents of their chamber pots into the street. Only a slow delivery man, bent such as me into his lone foul moods, finding himself an evening late on delivery, would be out, with his attention tethered to navigating clean ruts in the dark road.

She could not have been there long. She was dressed in a house coat, one that would be the sign of a lower post in domestic service, or the height of style in a proud working class home. The edges of it turned slightly up, but the modesty of it remained an open declaration. Her long fingers lay out like a daughter's accusations. I could see no outward marks of calamity. She seemed as calm as though napping in a fall meadow, with rain two days away from either side of the moment, and the lean clouds thrilling her into a remorselessly animal sleep.

I could have kept to my own business, but I live in the bowels of a lonely house and in the street by herself she seemed the fueling curd of loneliness and I thought: what is the harm? So I picked her up, folding her into the brace of my wheelbarrow, and turned back to my house, traveling no less like a man with a mission when I left it, the barrow then loaded with paid for salt. She jostled and giggled and burbled in the barrow like a cake of holiday jelly and one hand independently trailed off into the road and I let it draw a dust path alongside our travels. I noted how well she remained in the barrow, how little trouble she was, how convenient the geometry.

In my basement, she was cool and compliant and I made a place on one shelf where normally my buckets are bandaged or stored, and where sometimes the salt is spread out to be picked clean of impurities. To fold and unfold her was a joy. She was remarkably light and had not yet given into the rigidity the less faithful embrace. The smell of her was still an opulence of local oils and flowers, and the brine air of my cellar would hold her close for yet a few days; but I knew I would have to make my decisions soon, as my preservatives do not work by proxy, but directly.

I know the anchovy packers' arts, the careful work of women with delightfully small fingers who find in the fish what will halt the salt in its protection of the flesh; who know what to leave still in the pure anchovy for the product to remain identifiable as the product. I have seen them ladle in my salt, or the salt of my competitors, and embed the beautiful fish, press out the brine, break up the crystals that are too large. We sell our fine anchovies in farther lands than otherwise an anchovy could venture. We know how to keep anything you want, if you want it dear enough, from spoiling.

And so I worked.

I rearranged my work cellar. I set my buckets on other tables. I spread my salt on other platforms, picking it clean with light bent across new angles. Evenings I would talk to my salt-eyed companion and we quickly, near workmanlike, became comfortable with each other. All about our tiny space I could sense only the presence of salt, the remains of long years of industry, the product of the current day's travail. And I made my decision.

The magistrate came to my cellar to perform the ceremony, and my two witnesses were a rival saltman, with whom I was on good terms, and his huge and indelicate wife. It took the two of us to get this rival saltman's wife up and down the stairs to my cellar. She was in no way as pliant and carefree as my wife-to-be, and it is my understanding that she started the marriage as a handful of electricity, only to strike water and ground out early, then elapse into a bitter taste of sweet against the sodium chloride of her husband's quarreling house.

The truth is, my fellow saltman, as we waited to see if his wife might make an entrance without our assistance, asked me if I might be getting the better wife in the deal. All things taken aside, there are some attributes in a mate that might ease the chaffing of the salt trade, and some that might ring like a cut on the hand that must sort the salt, naked and thriving on pain.

The magistrate ended the service with the usual wish for many industrious children, but then grew nervous and left. In the interest of good manners, my fellow saltman and his wife, one stair at a time and with the huffing of trash fish left on the deck of a prize anchovy boat, soon followed.

In the weeks since, I have made no secret of my happiness. And I have made no secret of the fact that I am chronicling how a saltman encourages a wife into the seeming perfection mine has achieved. I have taken the well-worn steps that I applied from the anchovy packers' intricacies, noted where there is more to do when salting a wife, taken away what might be necessary with an anchovy but not with a spouse. I have refined the times of brine and salt and sunlight and air, and how to rub the skin so it does not go raw.

At first, saltmen and their wives would visit, making the obligatory rounds to the newlywed's house, bringing a gift of salt ham or salt pork or salt beef, or a cabbage cured in brine. Conversation would invariably slip into how my wife has remained so serviceable, so unchanging, so in need of only minor attentions and upkeep. I would regale my guests with the details, hold my wife's hand and speak glowingly of the art that seeded our love and keeps us forever the charring spice of each other's existence.

Soon it was more than the saltmen. Soon it was more than the hard bitten, labor cramped men of no means who wanted to know my methods. The old were followed by the young, the odd-jobs man by the ship's mate, the ship's mate by the ship's captain, the ship's captain by the sons of the anchovy merchants. I give them the tale of my marriage process, but the salt I sell.

THE MARKET

Sixteen children died in the attack. Two teachers were seriously wounded, but the placement of the explosive devices supports the conclusion that generating as much destruction as possible amongst the children was the terrorists' aim.

Any reason behind the tragedy is unexplained, and any information tying the perpetrators to the school, or to this play yard, is completely unknown.

But it does not have to be that way. Our firm retains some of the best historians and social scientists available. Many have been published in the finest academic journals, and mainline as tenured professors at important colleges and universities. Most have acted as analysts on national security projects, and undertaken customer analysis work for Fortune 500 companies.

Before you plant your first pipe bomb, or wrap your first shoe box of children's jacks in rat poison, we can compare the tangled lines of your ancestry with the expected ancestry of your intended victims, and come up with a precise historical intersection that will show that, at some point, your ancestors were oppressed by their ancestors. Enslaved, impoverished, massacred, insulted, maligned. It does not much matter. There is always something out there in the ethnic or racial memory. Our information reach goes back for centuries, even millennia.

Our huge database, along with our patented search engine - all guided by our unmatched team of liberal arts professionals - can find the appropriate point of vengeance, the wrong that must be righted. With customizable search parameters, we can shade the offense against any number of preferred outrages, provide a range of incidents across historical and geographical constructs, defend options based on age or sex or the numbers involved, and will develop sidebar projections detailing the anticipated impact of your selected rationale on any proposed audience.

Why be known for senseless violence, when, with a bit of up-front planning, you can be heralded for establishing justice? The fact that their people, twelve generations removed, wronged your people, twelve generations removed, changes every thing. Heroes are made with justifications, not with acts.

You do not have to do this alone. Without adequate preparation, eventually the public will question your motives. All your efforts might end up wasted: your need to make an open statement of principle could be seen as merely some lame, hopelessly ill-aimed comment about your lack of personal virility. You might soon be seen as the inadequate, misguided man whose one method of expression is violent imposition: the harvesting of fear for personal vindication.

The outcome can be brighter, the news releases more upbeat. A full package of our services will guarantee there is some sure-fire historically and socially relevant reason for your devastating actions. We will lay out the case, cite available references; we will even have our in-house essayist write you a manifesto decrying the packaged offense, if you select the deluxe version of our product.

Nothing can get any easier. In the end, all you have to do is kill.

CROWS' ALLEY

Do not think me special in any way. I am plain and well-used. I am unseen in an audience. I am as common a scarecrow as you can find in any southeastern Virginia garden worth the work of a scarecrow.

Many of the crows hardly notice me. The grackles perch on my arms, looking below for the shadow of likely food grazing at the edge of my penumbra: tiny, unthinking prey snatching anything excited by the emerging light. I pay them no attention: they have their work, and thus their utility.

I think of myself as pieces. My head constraint is a rice sack. My chest is held back by a shirt the farmer should have thrown out three years before he took it to make a limit to me. My arms feed into gloves that are tied to the sleeves of the shirt with old wire twisted together and folded over. I believe I would have stuffed my fingers less, as each hand looks like a balloon about to engage the higher air.

My pants the farmer outgrew longer ago than he can remember. Years he kept them in the closet, imagining one day he would slim back down to the strap of an action that once he was, the supple exclamation point he had intended to be all of his life. Too quickly the idea that he would return to his former electricity became the thought that he might one day, just possibly, reach back to be again what his past teased him with. And then the thought was that he was as he was, and it was entirely what he should be. And still the pants waited for good purpose. I was born to purpose, and so convenient to be bound by the pants, good or not.

Straw. Straw everywhere. The old cliché is that we scarecrows fear fire, and we do. But not as much as rot. Water in the straw and months of wet and dry and the straw begins to rot and sometimes to swell with

36

the dampness and we burst our buttons out of decay and not pride. The heavier straw falls out and if the farmer is not willing to rearrange the scarecrow we grow ever more limp and lean and like a line of cloth, a flag for crows and grackles and an embarrassment to our friends the owls and the ever-vigilant dangling silver pans.

Owls and pans and hawks and silver ribbon. Yes, I am but a member of a team. A scarecrow alone is not much deterrence. The owls assist with the rats; pie pans and pastry tins tied to the fence, or even tied to me, gambol in the wind and strike randomly against each other with sounds and whispers that seem to discourage the crows. Hawks master the high ether. Owls flick in and out of the dusk; pans twist in any slightly agitated air, scattering sun and catching the eyes of crows. Silver ribbons strain at the fence, flashing a much bigger mouth than it really has. Crows have many fields to select. I and my mates try to make this field a harder target than the neighbors' fields might appear to be.

It is simple work. I have few tricks to play, few tasks to complete. I am working by being what I am, nothing more. If I am here, I am on watch.

Nights I take off my hat and reach around to the nail just at the base of my neck, where stretched is the strap that supports me against this spike in the field. I slip myself cautiously off, dropping with nothing more than a rustle against the lazy leaves of my charge, the corn. I must say, for an ordinary scarecrow, I have kept my dexterity over the years. This farmer replaces my straw often enough that I always have a fresh crackle and a reach behind the neck that is the envy of all along this section of the county.

Scarecrows never sleep, so sometimes we gather at one farm, sometimes at another, swapping crow stories: laughing when one of us has been hit that day by crow droppings; describing the shadows of birds that seemed more bold than most, or faster. We talk shop late into the night - who saw the largest grackle this week, what the rain has done to our wardrobes, when the heat in the compost becomes smoke, how many times the Dozer farm has had its one cow stray into the field and disappear within the stalks. One scarecrow brings a rat he has domesticated and sometimes we feed the indolent rat parts of ourselves.

The rat has grown too fat to wander far and settles in at the knee of the owning scarecrow, as comfortable in our company as though he had been constructed not by God but by ordinary citizens.

Some nights I do not feel like company or shop talk and I will wander out of my field and up to the house. The farmer and his wife draw their curtains only part way, this land being in what is, these days, thought of as the essence of nowhere, though you can see the lights of the next house if you stand on the porch. I stand on the porch and see the lights of the next house. But mostly I look in at the farmer's windows as though I were watching a television play, wondering what is coming next and how it relates to what I have seen pass. Now and again I catch the farmer's wife fresh out of the shower, or sitting to align her hair, or trying on the night's sleeping wear - discarding this, selecting that, changing back. I imagine how rough my straw would be on her leathering skin, the sympathetic redness perhaps appealing and more deeply aligned to sensation: to actual awareness. I wonder if she would want to hear about my day, about the crows that ignore me and the ones that are terrified of the pans and the ones that avoid our field altogether, thinking me fierce. I could tell her things about the sun and the rain that she has not had the time to learn, nor the will to suffer. I could regale her with how well my good straw moves and holds form. I could speak of the eyes of owl and prey both at the moment of capture filled with exactly the same brilliant burst of planetary subduction.

I watch the farmer take his wife in his leathered arms, the better of him gone slack and the slack of him gone round. The top of his days are beyond him now and his horizons lie flat and snuggle comfortably with the ground. My end is sudden compared to his, but his is nonetheless relentless, mal-forming him as he struggles with time and season and the seeds of his next lumbering stretch of subsistence. He does not see in himself what his wife sees, nor does he look to see beyond the doing of things; and he bends into the light she gives, like he were the corn and she an elastic sun speckled with crowding clouds.

At the end of each night, I wander back to my stake in the field and wriggle my strap to jut just out so, and leap a few times until it catches, then angle and bob until I am fixed finally right on the pole. I am sure that, back at the house, the farmer drifting into his troubled rest is glad on some semi-conscious level that he did not fashion me complete: that I have only the outline of a man; that I am missing too many particulars to be useful in my intentions, and useless well beyond his intentions. I am what I am, and I spend the rest of the night thinking what I could be if I could have had a better maker, one who would have crafted the details as well as the outline. A maker unafraid to be nearly perfect in lovingly assembling even the unspoken unnecessary. A maker skilled enough to fashion a rival.

HOW THE COOP WAS BROKEN

The congress of kittens huddles in a corner of the chicken coop. Their mother is a polar bear, but, finding herself pregnant in a dicey environment, elected instead to bear kittens. Moving south was the difficult part.

Not all the kittens are hers, so there is an embedded social misconstruction: some are kittens of cat mothers, some are kittens of the polar bear mother. At least in the coop, the chickens cannot tell the difference; they sit at roost and think, well, now they are kittens and manageable, but, if they elect to stay, they will one day be cats and extraordinarily secular.

The congress cannot decide on what to decide since it has not decided on parliamentary procedures. Overhead, the thermals are practicing disdain and it is still possible that the congress will be irrelevant, perhaps even the kittens.

The chickens hope so. The kittens would be more manageable independently.

I am outside trying to reason with the polar bear. The door is too small. It is not a commercial coop. Let the kittens be your eyes. The bear smooths the house dress she put on just for this occasion, trying to stay between me and the body of the woman who was mauled for the dress.

I am simply trying to sell the farm.

I want the railroad to come through and make me rich. I could not care less whether the kittens can get their rafter of procedures ratified and move on, but I want to include them in the sale, perhaps have them itemized.

I cannot let the polar bear know.

The kittens who belong to the bear are beginning to see religion as the alternative. They spin in one corner of the coop and stop communicating with the others. Every so often they count themselves, thinking they know the sacred number of kittens the polar bear bore.

For the moment, the polar bear and I are laughing at twice-told jokes. Getting along famously is my specialty. I think I have this all wrapped up and ever more of my attention is devoted to listening for the locomotive, seeing tracks in the melon mounds.

And when the sun is shining as full as a laundry line on the kittens' efforts to build a ritual, the chickens with hawk feathered talons and timepiece beaks come rugby down shouting NOW.

I cannot hold the polar bear back.

THE MERMAID'S SON

As with most things, I thought nothing of it until it got in the way. By then, I had already learned to move it about, flip it up when it began to inconveniently drag, smooth it back when I needed a clear angle to sit. But, eventually, it began to get ungainly in a standard pair of trousers, and so I had to take stock of it.

It was not un-cute, given the way that it connected. The whole of it seemed remarkably willing to fit in, at least for a fluke, and I could hardly blame it for its bulk. It would have to be an awful bother to any sort of uneventful clothing that might be caught expecting only two legs.

The simple thing was to cut a hole for it. The trouble is that the end connecting to flesh, and the end that was meant to pound water, are of different sizes; and once I cut a hole big enough for the fin itself, the hole gapped miserably loose at the connecting end, and I might as well not be trying to wear pants at all.

The solution was to clothe myself in only those baggy but elastic half pants that proved so popular a season or so ago with kids that wanted to look ghetto. You could almost stuff a small fishing vessel into the legs of one of those pairs of shorts; so, accepting an oversized fit, I could put both a leg and the tail through one shorts leg, hike the clothing leg up a bit, and, while it was a little awkward, I was covered.

As my new merman's tail grew, I could do more things with it. It had its own set of muscles, its own commitments to symmetry. I could amuse myself for hours seeing how far away from its main axis I could spin it; how much of a spiral I could curl it in; how much force against the air could I stretch into the fin and then, with a sickening flick of my rattling spine, hurl teasingly forward.

This was a symbiosis. As the tail grew, I used it ever more eloquently, and for my ever closer-to-continual use the tail grew stronger. And a stronger tail I would use more often, find new uses for, strengthen. The tail would curl around the leg it had been mated to by the expedience of my shorts, trying to stay out of the way as I walked, and even with this effort growing thicker, more tendon and less scale, more tendon and less flesh, more tendon and less fickleness.

I took it one day to the beach, and it uncoiled radiantly from my leg, large enough now to lay its fluke flat on the sand. I guessed enough not to go too close to the water: but there was a boy, who had never seen a man with a merman's tail before, who brought a sand pail of ocean water inland to me and poured it slowly over the relaxed fluke. The leather webbing oscillated in self-luxuriance. The boy ever so slightly ran his elfin fingers along the fluke's supporting spines and I could feel the alien density of his touch: fiercely, dutifully in the thought bubbles of my mid-brain.

The tail now is large enough to support me; and some mornings, before I can get balanced again on my petty legs, it will bound with me around the house; and more than once, without me consciously opening the door, it has slipped into the front yard. I tell it to wait, wait until I get my pants, but it will stop only to wick the dew left in the grass and then off we will go. Once, we made it to the fence before I could rock into a two footed stability and lift the tail out of its preferred balance, shaming it into curling for emotional comfort again about my leg.

I know what is coming. Even I stare longingly down the length of my street, imagining the left turn, then right, that puts me on the path to the ocean. I feel a mounting greed deep in my heart as the four chambers begin ever so slyly to reorient themselves and my scaly skin dries unwillingly in the suddenly thick air. I will not be able to stop the tail forever. This last week I have been eating fish, fish and crabs and shrimp, and I am ready, oh I am ready. But I have my legs, and I can run. I can run! I can still run to the ocean. In great, land-gravity shattering steps, the tail but a rudder behind me, I can run! I can run with the smell of the ocean reeling me in, the sound of feet dimming in sand, in water becoming indistinguishable from the sound of a fluke, a fluke taking its aim and turning to its brother legs: my turn! It is my turn!

SATIN SHEETS

The sensor had been set to vibrate when she was detected: and it was clocking his pocket, sending a shimmer through his pants, radiating into the flesh of his thigh, and coming out as a dull thought whimpering in the bone. He had been told she would be in this bar, at this time, but things can go wrong: other patterns might intervene, some other curious plan might have cut across this one - and then again, she does have a will of her own. No matter how predictable she might be, no matter how much detail one puts into ordering a course of events, free-will can crash a good plan like rogue salvers harvesting the car you are still making payments on.

But she was here. And close. The air was filled with her.

He had been sitting there a while, appearing to be absorbed in his view screen. To the workday world he looked like another random idle man, unwilling to go home and parked in the bar for lack of a better place to be. When the sensor went off, he took a second to organize himself, to conceal his happy reaction. He ran the length of his hand across the synthetic wood table that he had selected after several trial runs, one with a good view of the main serving and seating area. He commenced counting, to quiet his breath. He tapped his thumb on the slightly raised table edge. And then cautiously he glanced up to look about the lightly lit, dismally scattered room.

There were about forty people of all makes and models lingering about the recesses and edges of the bar; but he picked her out immediately with only an unfocused shrug. She was at the middle banister of the bar, seeming by her presence to divide it into separate halves: an alluring eye-stop, consuming every bit of her chair, all six foot five inches of her at home in the utilitarian furniture.

Carefully he squeezed the pheromone tablet waiting in his pocket between the nails of his thumb and forefinger, expecting the scent to be held up only momentarily by the cloth of his pants. He kept his hand flat, trapping the scent, not wanting to blast the room with the compound - preferring that it lift slowly and insinuate itself spectrally, sluggishly, almost reluctantly, into the atmosphere.

Her thin, lengthy arms were all scale, but she had a woman's feet and only from the ankle to her mid thigh did her small blue-green scales layer over one another. Above, there was quickening tan skin, disappearing into the siren of her skin-tight mini-skirt. Scales were feathered throughout her midsection, but did not predominate. Her form-fitting top seemed to mechanically caress what must have been purely human breasts. The scales on her neck were smaller, and tapered into her short auburn hair. Her head, maybe a bit more angular than a raw-born woman's head, nonetheless held all the usual human features in all the right numbers and orders and general positions.

There. There was just the tiniest flick of her narrow tongue, as the pheromone began to work through the room, reaching out to her alone, and she flipped almost autonomically a taste of the smell to her school-child's nose.

She was good work. The best he had ever seen. He, himself, had done some fine work, but nothing like this. You would say she was pure Manila. The Manila plant had done the best work about, but in the sterilization scandal the Manila plant had been nuked by United Bio International. Nearly twelve million people lost, as well as perhaps twenty million sub-hominid creations, and the contents of more than one hundred patents. Six years later, some of the processes Manila was using have not yet been recreated. You would think someone would have stolen the patents.

She looked around, obviously beginning to feel the scent. She would have no idea why she was getting an edge, why the evening was sharpening this quickly. Even though the synthetics were, by law, sterile, most of them still had the capacity to react to sexual stimuli. She was reacting. A shoulder slithered up and then tartly around. The small of her back receded noticeably. In a slow, serpentine way, her chest inched forward and up. Her mixture of DNA was coming out with its own plan for the scent that was working its wicked way into her multi-species libido.

Manila was gone, and everyone's creations were sterile. There would be no letting them mate to come up with improved models all on their own. That is what Manila had done, creating unpredictable work, adding her, letting nature take its course there, and ultimately suffering for it.

All of the synthetics pumped into society, still with all their hybrid creation equipment, but none of it working - well, except maybe in one clandestine case. One smuggled synthetic, rumored in the literature, capable of merging the synthetic manufacturing process with the miracle of unlicensed procreation biology. Maybe just one left. Just possibly, after a year of underground research work and video manipulations and falsified bio scans and stolen documents and bribes and faked identity chips: maybe one got through the filters. And he was hoping to soon find out.

Yes, she looked pure Manila. And the rumor of the legendary quality Manila put out got more precise every year that Manila was history. But she could not be Manila. Manila was gone. He would have to get over it, just like everyone in the business would have to get over it.

He got up, figuring she had tasted enough of the pheromones and that with her over-saturation, he would not seem too obvious a pheromone hot spot. He smoothed his pants to clear some of the scent from his hand. He half attempted to clear the excitement from his eyes. He tried to walk like business was his pleasure. He measured the seconds of his breath and worked his shoulders back slowly. He did not want to look like prey.

"Excuse me, but I could not help but notice how wonderfully well put together you are."

She tipped a foot back on one of her six inch heels and looked around at him. Her eyes preceded the movement of her face and as her head came around, the eyes re-centered themselves from the far right. It was almost as through there were an outer skin and an inner skin, and that it took a while for the outer skin to catch up.

"Jason Thumbold. I am a bio engineer, and my hobby is snakes. So, naturally, I could not help but notice you."

She did not seem to differentiate what might be scientific interest from what might be the hope for a quick trip to one of the private rooms. The length of her played out and she seemed to compress into a coil.

"Satin Verdith. Yes, a man who makes snakes would probably notice me."

She had to have been the product of at least a year's growth and splicing. Tray upon tray of bio matter, and magnetic molds precise down to the pico-micron obeying holographic designs. Each technician an artist, and even the people who manage the room temperature aware of each hundredth of a degree. Her arms and legs had human joints, though the arms were a bit out of proportion - surely for some balance dynamic and not aesthetics - though she still looked far more human than snake; but you could tell that in her backbone there was slither, and there would be some jointing mathematics that he had never encountered - never having tried to include slither and strut in the same chassis.

Manila. But Manila was gone. Who did this work? He had not been told, and wasn't originally curious, but he was now. United Bio, or Asia-Tech? Or maybe a consortium? Or an unknown government lab anchored at the edge of the continental shelf. It did not matter, did it?

Her tongue flicked in the air again, drawing in the scent of him. By now, to her the room would be a blur of pheromone. Sex would be shouting in the sweep of her ears. Sex would be burning along the sides of her thighs. He would be one spot of heat in a field of heat. The brightest spot.

Her memory flash would have been as laborious as her bio assembly. A team of neural scientist would have tripped memory and learning down to the synapse level, testing and retesting the speed of ion exchange, mapping ideas to locations, implanting methods. She had a sassy, sensuous nature that would have taken weeks to burn in. As much work would have gone into her mind as a civic team puts into to creating a master chip set to run a medium sized city.

"I've been building them for years. I like to see what I can get the basic form to do. Sort of stretch the physical limits of the natural ingredients. I keep most of the prototypes as pets. The neighbors worry when I work too long that I might leave a lab unlocked." She was not about to laugh at small talk, and he did not expect her to. He was looking at her fangs. Retractable.

She noticed the object of his interest. "Oh, don't worry. No venom. I have a full set of teeth, and, frankly, these just get in the way. I can't think of when I last let them out." She dipped forward, and her breasts lolled a little in the form-fitting top; he could see that she had nipples - maybe a tad bit large, but that could have been the fetish of the fellow who grew those breasts. Most bio engineers add something into the mix that isn't in the design, but which they would like to see if they were going to purchase the creation. It can be an occupational hazard.

He did not know how much she knew about the effects of the pheromones on her. Her licking in the scent with her tongue may have been pure unconscious reaction. Or she might have consciously known why she was tipping ever closer to the edge of action, why the whole of her seemed to be wasting into purpose, why she was drawing in the scent and becoming a consequence of its frolics through her system.

"No venom, but I bet you could leave a nice puncture wound." She looked away and then back, letting him know she had left a few puncture wounds, though he could not be sure if it were in play or in anger. "But what really astounds me are these scales. They look purely reptilian, but up close they seem to have moisture, texture. I bet to the touch they are less like scales, more like feathers." He leaned in as close to her shoulder as he dared.

"Oh, go ahead. See for yourself." Her voice was less of a lilt and wavered towards the rasp, no doubt due to the narrowness of her tongue and the split at the end. But it rang of human sensibilities, human needs, human invitations.

So he reached out ever so gently and stroked the upper part of her arm. Softly, in a spiral he traced the edge of one of her scales and drifted ever so playfully, cautiously to the next. He could see her hips tighten and there was but the sense of a shudder in her shoulder, the inhumanly long sinews through her torso tensing ever so tenuously, and he thought now, now, now, now.

"I'd really like for you to see what I can do with scales. These are so soft they seem almost like a foreskin. I'd like to have you run your fingers over some of my work." He drew a small whorl on the meat of her triceps. "My place is just a couple of miles out of town. We can leave your car here, take mine, and I'll bring you back in time for a nightcap."

Pheromone tablets make everything so easy. Did she know that? Did she know that the secret, kept even from her, which hopefully was stumbling blindly to its own conclusions inside her, might make her a better victim for the snake pheromone than any other reptile mix?

Rather than answer, she stood, passing her credit chip over the nearby receptacle, tapping a confirmation of the bill, and looked down at him, waiting with a look of conclusion and beginning. Waiting for the end and start of absolutely anything.

It took him a moment to realize he had to lead her out of the bar and to his car. With her natural height, and her perilously high heels, she towered over him, but it was his car they were going to, so he had to turn and begin to thread the two of them through the unconcerned crowd and out of the side parking lot entrance. He took half a second to glance about to ensure that no one was taking special notice of them. These pairings occur all the time. Nothing abnormal here. Nothing for anyone to keep track of. Just a man picking up a half-snake, half-woman unaccompanied synthetic at the bar on a slow night. No one should care.

As the car auto-piloted them to his place, he was stroking the flat of her thigh, remarking how the transition from skin to scale was so smooth, how design and workmanship had to go hand in hand for an idea to turn out so splendidly. Her tiny mini-skirt had hiked up even farther and, had she not been warm blooded despite her snake additions, they would have had to max out the car's air conditioning to keep her from frying herself.

As the car pleasantly parked itself he felt her tongue on the back of his neck and knew no one was going to be looking at his latest engineering designs tonight: so he dropped all pretense and straight from the garage they went up the elevator to his sleeping quarters, one of her legs - more rubbery than he had thought - wrapped double about his as the elevator whispered by each floor. In his unruly bed, he learned she had at least five joints he had not expected; and when she slipped her discs she became serpentine in movement, able to slip her ankles together and clasp her hands and slither about the room on her belly and on her side - then snap her discs back into place and stand to walk sensuously about the room. Even her most mundane move was seduction. By design, she could do no less than give men reasons to plot erections.

It was the best work he had ever seen.

He found himself following her lead. He was quite happy to be her object tonight, and he marveled at her twists and turns and unsubtle suppleness, and he felt he had let her down when he had to end, at least for a while, his full participation. His exhaustion was a precursor to what he would welcome tomorrow as human limbs taken too far past tolerances and muscles happily pushed out of bounds. He gave thanks there were better engineers out there than he, and that they had produced this.

In the morning, she slept heavily on the side of his bed that he had not seen so majestically filled often enough. She would never admit it, but just the tips of her fangs had slipped forward, edging conspiratorially out to rest against her lower lip. Quietly, he reached up and turned on the bio scanner sewn into the canopy of his bed and let it silently run the length of her. Mechanically unconcerned, it silkily shunted back and forth, layering images three dimensionally in the small view port. And, yes, there it was. Small, from its recent and hopelessly wonderful activation, but it was there nonetheless. She was the one. The rumors had not been false; the secret possibilities had not been a set up by the authorities to act as a trap. Her reproductive system sang inside of her. She had been the one smuggled out. She had been the one not sterilized.

Did she know? Probably not. Did it matter? Not at all.

They had timed it right. Slowly dividing and reforming and growing even now, the tangle of genetic mix that would become her clutch of eggs was gathering itself. Just a small microscopic blot now. It was hard to tell when she would drop them, given the mixed biology, but she would have a brood of the hard shelled little ones to keep warm, waiting for the hatch.

Each one of those eggs would be worth millions on the black market. Even United Bio International would be willing to pay whatever anyone else offered, plus ten percent insurance, if only to take them and put them on ice in the basement. But the idea that cross-breed eggs existed would be a blow to the monopolies. And the team that produced these eggs would, from someplace unknown and in someway torturous - if they could keep from getting made quite dead - get paid millions and millions and quietly retire to one of the reclaimed zones in an unknown city to live like corporate kings.

He put on his shirt, and Satin Verdith in her sleep let go a mild, seductive hiss while her tongue flicked reflexively. She coiled on her side, the sheets bunched behind her and keeping her rolled in one direction, her body a knot of scale and skin and her inability to sweat the thing about her that lasted a while with Jason Thumbold. For him, she was in ways so human, in ways so manufactured. He thought to wake her to see if any of the pheromone rage - so blind and wonderful-ly feral last night - or perhaps some real affection, lasted dearly enough for her to fold about him again this morning in elastic ecstasy. But no, he admitted to himself with a releasing coil of longing — he had to go downstairs and make all that unneeded artificial insemination equipment appreciably look as though it had been recently used.

THE MARRIAGE OF THE FLAT MAN

I forgot about him for two days. That is not surprising, considering the misted alcohol stupor I led myself into after first running in to him. I called in sick to work and slept for a day and a half, letting the solace work its way out of my ashamed, frightened body. I reminded myself of the rum cakes of my childhood, the ones mother would let me have but a small piece of on holidays. My imagination of inebriation was far less toxic than the realities I later discovered. And here, after first running in to him, I shot the wad and put on my first two day drunk.

After first running into him. I was not looking where I was going. I do not know where my mind was. I was fumbling with the sash on my coat. Or maybe I was rambling on my cell phone. Or I was counting cracks in the sidewalk. Whatever I was doing, it was stunningly unremarkable. And I turned the corner at full pace and there he was. I saw him only after I full force smacked into him. A blur of a man even then: even as we tried to occupy unsuccessfully the same space. Until I made physical contact, he was unknown to me, unimportant to me, not a part of my landscape. One of millions who inhabit the earth for which I have no category.

But after we hit, complete with the sudden halt to our progress, he and I stepped rudely apart, momentarily merely two halves of a serendipitous collision. His eyes widened like those of a bird in a tempest. Perhaps the belt latch on my coat was sticking out. Or there was a capped pen in one of my pockets angled forward. Or my impractical stiletto heel hit the inside of his ankle. From that fog of my life existing before our striking face to face, I could assemble no cause.

But I heard the hiss of air. The even paced, tunneling sound. I saw the candied look of amazement in his trapped eyes.

Without a word, he quickly began to shrink; and from the folding of loosened skin on skin, I could not tell where the breach was. The hiss came and went as his body wiggled and wriggled and slowly began to come down: shortening, and then narrowing, then shortening, then folding, then dipping cautiously over into a wash basket heap; his face, that had started barely above mine when we stood in the first half second of our meeting, lay flat on the collapsed bounty of his body and clothes, looking awash with astonishment up at me.

I knew no social norm for this. I had no etiquette to tell me what to do. I had never so soundly deflated an unknown man before. What to do; what to do? Feeling near criminal, I stuffed him into my oversized purse, looked about for witnesses, and ran as gracefully as I could in my brusque heels home, where I placed him on a shelf in the bedroom and cracked open the bottle of bourbon that kept me for two days without memory of what I had unwillingly done.

But I got my senses back, fishing them from the spirited cesspool of my self-blame and self-pity, netting myself back into the moment, the second, the minute, the hour, the day. My hopelessness of responsibility had gotten the better of me; but I was in some ways a victim of incidental randomness as much as he. But I had not deflated. I was not sitting wadded on an unknown woman's closet shelf.

With my reason resettled, and my faith set right again, I quite respectfully pulled him from the closet and laid him out carefully on the bed. He was unabashedly wrinkled from two days on the shelf, and I tried to smooth him out without cracking his surfaces. He seemed to like this, and he smiled, but I could only draw him out to half his original height and width, and he looked like a smirking midget of himself, a two dimensional representation of what he would have been had he been born an elf, or a bridge troll. I selfishly felt less sorry for him - he, looking now as he did - but I was sated with the responsibility I had for his current condition, and I was awash with mission.

I looked over him for the disembodying hole I had apparently caused. I suspected a tear would be evident, a discoloration of the skin, a bit of fabric turned out from where his pants and shirt and shoes had all shrunk with him. Maybe a button dipping curiously sideways; or what would appear to be a mole which, on closer inspection, would be a blow through of his forearm; or perhaps an anonymous cicatrix on his cheek.

When I could find nothing on his front, I turned him over and spread him out again, feeling along the shoulders and stretching out his calves, twisting through the small of his back and looking inside his pants pockets. I ran my hands along every inch of him, and I swear I heard him giggle; though without air he could not have done so. But I could feel him smiling. A slow burn of a smile; one that bungles about in closets and ends up on window ledges. A smile that is proud of itself for its industry. A smile that noiselessly smacks the air unlucky enough to be around it.

I imagined him the sort of man who did not usually garner the attention of women. I do not know why. I do not remember him as being particularly without charm or looks in his inflated state; though nothing of decisive substance could be learned from his disengaging air-removed condition. But I felt the hollow hum of his appreciation even in the limp folds of his empty skin, in the simple flat of his airlessness. His smile - no, grin - followed me even when I turned him face down and inspected the back of his head, though I could not have punctured him there.

After twice inspecting him front and back, after feeling all of him with first the fingers and then the flat of the hand, I decided that I would make no progress until I could get him partially inflated and look for the part of him that was spitting back air. It works with inner tubes. It works with beach balls. It would have to work with a man.

But I did not know where the inflation valve might be. I had found no hole that let the air out; but, at the same time, I had found no valve to allow the push of air in. I looked for something convenient. I experimented with the fingers, to no success. And I tried the toes, but nothing would enter. I worked down his fly, uncoiled his sexual relevance, and tried that; and while he smiled wider than he had ever before, still nothing inflated, not even the organ itself, and the air I tried to force in just leaked across the scrotum and uselessly away. He tossed at me that broad smile which I was coming to experience as a briny mocking lecture, and I started to wish I would find no valve, no way to re-inflate this ever more insufferable man.

In the end, I sat in the wing-backed chair that I have kept in the darkest corner of my bedroom for years, and considered the man that I had, as a fully accidental consequence of an unbidden random encounter, deflated. He lay across my bed, a bare ten feet away, staring at the ceiling - since I had turned him again over on his back - with his irritating, ineffective little goblin's smile slowly fading. I could see a wrinkle here or there across the fallow skin and the ordinary clothes the man had become stuck in when he deflated: when the air left him and I had smuggled him in my purse into my home and into my bedroom, and then onto the shelf of my closet; and then to my bed, where I ministered to him no less faithfully and prudently than would a nurse minister to a favored dying family member. I am doing my part.

I sat breathing unconsciously for a while. And then I began to breathe consciously. And I thought: breath. Breath. Perhaps taking in air and holding it as though it were a religion is as much a matter of will as it is of tears and rips and valves and any force employed to externally force air in. Taking in air is what a man does because he wants to. Holding air is what a man does because he has will. Why doesn't this man have a want to accept ordinary air? Why doesn't this man have the will to hold atmosphere, to roll it about within him for the profits buried in oxygen and nitrogen? Why was I trying to force air into a man who would not hold air on his own, who imagined himself punctured by a chance encounter with a random distracted woman? What responsibility did I imagine I had? I could be so foolish.

And was that encounter random? How did I know that he had not been waiting there, just around the corner, waiting for someone who looked gullible, who would instantly believe that she had some responsibility for the demise of a complete stranger, perhaps a stranger who was already deflating and was simply holding on, holding on until some rube with the look of saintliness or fear or responsible sociability stumbled blindly around the corner and became his mark.

What if I were the victim?

And then, just barely at the limit of sound, I muttered "Water"; and joyously, triumphantly, I could see on the man's flat and empty face the bare beginnings of a stingy frown. He knew. Oh, he knew. I watched slyly from my chair, my sight of him angled, seeing enough that I could learn the broad measures of his emotions and his anxieties. Yes, I was learning. Perhaps water. Dumping him in the tub and seeing where the liquid rushed in. If he did not need air, how could he drown? The water would rush in and then I could pick him up and see from where it rushed out. And if that did not work, I would think of something else. There would always be something else to think of. I would be everlasting in my efforts, I would be dogged. I would administer every test and trial and relentlessly seek out the flaw that let him go flat. Whether I had caused that flaw or not. Whether either of us could profit from the fixing of the flaw. But I would know, I would know all!

I rose and stepped lightly over to the bed, where with minutely measured movements I rolled him gently into a compact cylinder of outline, the man flattened and without air, making room for myself on the bed.

I regarded the coming long, luxurious months of education and experimentation, of discovery and mastery, that shimmied before me in my wide and breathless dreams: waiting like velvet servings of rum cake; and not just mother-sized sniffles of rum cake, but who cares, here-have-another-slice, portions. Soon I would know everything, everything, everything. Silly man who could hold no air, there would be no secrets denied me.

ADJUSTMENT

"This one fits nicely into its shoebox sized recharger, and during the day's charging cycle makes absolutely no noise at all." The salesman's belief was electric. "With the device able to exit from the charger from all sides, you can wedge the apparatus just about anywhere, and as long as one face has clear access, the robot can get in and out cleanly." The efficiency of it seemed to have just struck him. His eyes did a bit of a side shimmy and refocused on the carefully listening customer. "Stacked in with shoes and shoeboxes and sweaters and belts and toys on the floor, no one would think it might be anything that wasn't supposed to be there." The salesman leaned one hand on the wall, practicing his hard won practicality, just as he had seen in his two most recent sales training holograms.

"Well, it is very nice." Mr. Tittles, John Tittles, bent a bit at the knees to look the offered model straight on. It was not an imposing device. Just like a shoebox. The size and look and geometry of it he could understand; the insides, those were another matter. Hopefully, a curative family matter.

"Good lines and easy access. Quiet. Only you know it is there." Price was going to be the problem. Price is always the problem. How much? Oh, do not ask that until you are sold.

"You don't think it is a little small?" John Tittles was still bending, staring into the perfectly featureless short face of the box that acted both as cover and recharger for the barely twelve by four inch automaton. His hair settled uncared for across his forehead, and a brief wisp of discomfort stitched across his back, his body being angled just a few millimeters out of its usual lines.

"It's not the size that matters. This unit has the best adaptable, self-programming module available." As though this customer might know whether it was top-of-the-line in these features or not. "It has a wireless connection that will download any advances in the science and incorporate them into that very night's program. It feeds off of each encounter's outcome and rethreads its approach, ensuring both safety and stimulation." It learns just what quivers the skin and puts starch in the toes. "You can get fancier, you can pay more, but you can't get better. This will do all that you want it to do." The salesman was leaning slightly over, beside John Tittles, staring into the same blank face of the recharger, wondering what John Tittles was seeing, what there was to be seen for John Tittles in this faceless slick of metal housing. Perhaps, from the dark behind the charging case door, the robot was staring back.

"What's the boys' name?" Not that the salesman cared, but it redirects the sales approach. It takes the conversation away from models and features and back to why the concerned father came in to this store in the first place.

"John, Jr." Junior. The practice was coming back, but usually with a more uncommon name. Being a junior with a name like John would put the boy two steps back to start with. His mother would probably call him John Junior, and the boy would begin to wrap around that name like bunting in a bicycle's spokes by the time he was ten.

"Well, Mr. Tittles, you've seen how children have turned out for the last few years. Unimaginative. Captive to the 3-D video. Apolitical, or uncompromisingly radical. It has been a sad state. Listless citizens. Many of them can't hold a job. I wonder myself if I can ever retire: no one to replace me. With all these kids coming of working age and simply stumbling out of the academies with no freshness of thought, no evolution of how to use the information they have collected - no spark of imagination - those of us left from the last generation might have to stay on the job forever. It's sad, sad, sad." Well, not so sad if the commissions stay high, or they start augmenting sales with a base salary.

"I know. I don't want my boy to end up like that." No. John Tittles could not abide the idea. A boy with maybe an advanced degree in genetics unable to come up with two original thoughts to mate together; no initiative, living at home with a mom and a dad that themselves end up working ten years into what should have been retirement just to keep a roof over his head - and he with no thought that things could be different. Existence. Eat, sleep, find the restroom. Eat. Sleep. Exist. Eat. Sleep. Why?

"If you start young enough, maybe you can spark some deep questioning, some adaptive reasoning, get him thinking outside of the easy and available." Maybe the boy would begin to think his life worthy of his own involvement. "Perhaps you can grow the magical." That is a line that brings them back to their usually unfounded belief that anything could fix their lackluster child.

The salesman stood up, knowing this would be the sign to Mr. Tittles that Mr. Tittles, John Senior, should stand up too — and that he should come to a conclusion. After all, Mr. Tittles would not be the only customer of the day. What other sales opportunities might be missed if too much of a salesman's slick and sly grappling-hooks were wasted on one customer? The time to close the deal had come.

"I guess you are right. And this model would fit nicely in the back of his closet."

"I think you will see that you are doing the right thing. You won't regret it, and, years from now, John Junior will thank you for it." If this small episode does not get lost in all of the other grander, louder, more dangerous episodes that are to come. "You can't give a boy anything better than a healthy imagination." The poor man, wrapped around being a better father, imagining his son made new into a Titan amongst his thick-headed mates, did not know that he could haggle price, that the posted price was only a starting point. The salesman's commission would go up for getting full list out of the gullible customer. So few customers show any imagination, show any initiative; but usually, on price, the basic greed and value instincts kick in. Not here. John Tittles was a man on a mission.

The salesman walked the satisfied new purchaser to the counter, where the paperwork was already laid out. The concerned father passed his credit card over the reader, inspected the amount, and signed the release of liability required in the sale of any automated closet monster.

He did not read it; no one does. Finally, John Tittles took the already assembled model under his arm and turned to hurry to the omnitrack train, to make sure he could get home and install the tapping, wheezing, calling beast-in-the-dark at the back of John Junior's closet before the boy and his mother got home from their cybernetics-design exercise class.

That very night, the boy, hovering at the border of sleep, would be innocently discovering the monster in the closet. The boy's thin and underfed imagination would perk up at the rapping in the dark, the barely believable breathing, and the name almost called at the edge of hearing. His mind would race - John Tittles, Senior was hoping - right out of its drab habits and be off like a rabbit trying to outrun the memory of wolves. Nothing can spark an imagination like the fear for one's soul that a nameless closet monster puts into you. Tittles, Senior, thought: my son, the engineer; my son, the physicist. That boy needs the smug scared out of him. That boy needs something unfound to ponder. That boy needs.

One closet monster it will be.

A TIME FOR RIO

I met her at the Ninth Annual Progressive Poultry Convention in New Henbridge. It was being held at the local Comfort Inn, and, since there was no conference room, everyone was milling about in the reception area or loitering in the parking lot and I bumped into her while trying to get past the fake fountain and through the open glass door.

She was taller than I, and was the only woman there wearing heels. Poultry women usually wear flats; even when they dress up they tend to put on those sawed off heels that you see on a child's sandals. Poultry women are practical: they have to get from point A to point B on their feet, and they have to be able to out-maneuver their stock, so they tend to stay with the serviceable. Even at dress up, show-myself-off, events like this. You can't hide the fact that pragmatism excites you; that what works, works. Appearance doesn't get the coop hosed out.

It is all about what the poultry thinks, not what your competition will believe.

When I pulled up short not to knock her completely over, I nearly dropped the plastic room cup I had brought with me, then poured too full with vending machine diet Pepsi. When I righted myself, I realized I was looking straight ahead at the crease where her neck joined her body and I thought: this is a tall woman.

She did not have the look of a poultry person. Her long lines did not bode well for hauling feed in hundred pound sacks, or driving a mini-tractor between angled coops. You would have a hard time imagining her with a square tipped shovel, making the most out of poultry poop: dropping low with the shovel blade flat and scraping along the concrete, her full weight behind it pushing, the waste rolling up and over the lip to slip into the shovel base.

Even though my wife never comes to these events, I figured this woman must be here with one of the agribusiness people: the wife of one of those in the upper strata who are either looking to sell in bulk contracts, or looking to buy in bulk contracts. Those people bet on prices going up and again on prices going down, on both good seasons and avian flu, and somehow year after year they make money. We smaller operators don't know how they do it. We think in terms of feed prices and better poultry wire and how to get to market faster and the bank officers, who don't know poultry from cattle, breathing down our necks like insatiable chicken hawks. Yes, she had the look of one of these, with legs that actually went up as high as you could want and a chest that fit alluringly - and as if it were natural to do so - in the overly elegant dress she had picked for the event.

I guess she had gone into the parking lot to escape the crush in the reception area. She held an actual glass slightly forward and tipped the whole draught of her body marginally to the side. No doubt her husband had stock options and was down one of the hallways, bent conspiratorially over with a quietly nodding brood, intentionally confusing some small operator like me and getting a bid price that no one not overly impressed with the gravity of this event would ever agree to.

"You needed some air, too".

She had spoken like the soft coo of a hen at first laying. Just from the sound, I could imagine feathers hackling, a slight adjustment of the withers, and a settling comfortably in. I must have looked up with a sense of wonder, or confusion, pasted on my face.

"Rio. Rio McWeathers."

And she held out her diaphanous, marathon hand, which I pumped like one of those small commuter car jack cranks. Her handshake was a man-like handshake, the hand turned sideways like a man's; not the dainty over the top grab-my-fingers woman's shake, but a palm to palm, let's swap dirt, handshake. I thought, maybe, just maybe, she had in the past tossed a plug of poultry manure here or there, could ride a tractor seat with overused suspension, all while proving she had been poured into her starched coveralls.

"You here for the convention?" I asked, as though anyone would be at this Comfort Inn in New Henbridge for any other reason. And, if they had wandered in on this convention, why on earth would they be out in the parking lot with thirty dedicated poultry farmers, each smelling still of poultry blood, no matter how many baths they had taken, nor how long in the hot tub they had sat admiring the bubbles, and no matter how much cheap bourbon they had smuggled in to this otherwise dry affair?

My name. My name? I thought about giving my name only later. At that moment, I would have had to peck it off of my driver's license, or look inside the lapel of my coat where the wife hides it in case the laundry confuses me with someone else.

"I came in last night. Drove almost sixteen hours straight. Just had time to drop out on the bed, come out of the nap to change into my day suit, and slide straight from breakfast here." Her mouth moved as though it had things to do and this was one of those things, as silky as a rooster just before dawn.

She was talking as though she were talking to me. Not at me. Not over me. Not even with me. But to me. As though I might actually need to know what she was telling me. I could see her neck move and occasionally I would look up to see her nostrils barely quiver and then I would catch the bottoms of her eyes.

"That's my car over there. The little blue one."

There were three or four little blue cars over there, but it did not matter that I could not actually pick out which was hers. I could imagine any one of them as her car. I could select the one which best fit my version of the magical events of her driving, of her edging her long body perfectly into the driver's seat and fondling the steering wheel as though making it happy were the key to a good drive. And if one car fell short mid-imagination, I could simply select another car: swing the door differently, or feel the upholstery pull at her backside with a different anger, and I could unabashedly crowd faux-rooster deeper into my black and white fantasy.

"Nice car, but a long drive either way." I said. And I thought it was a good observation. Any one of the cars would be nice, if she had sat in it for sixteen hours straight. Each would have all that any consumer would need, and every one would reek of new car smell and hold flocks of social upward mobility. I could drive a car like that for days, stopping only for gas, kidneys happily throbbing and my mouth as dry as the poultry yard in July.

"I was so tired I left half of my luggage in the trunk last night." Oh, my joy at the thought! First, there was no husband on this trip, as surely he would not leave his wife's luggage in the trunk overnight. A woman like that would have expensive tastes and her obliging husband would keep a close eye on her possessions, making sure they were accounted for and not left out where they could be collateral damage in some other unpredicted destructive act. Second, there were no bell hops here, no front desk staff. The girl who had checked me in was all alone at the counter, leaning in her white shirt on the brushed rock and glass, her jeans thick and moving against her like they did not get much exercise. That girl would be carrying no one's luggage, would probably not even replace the luggage cart. In fact, I think I saw the luggage cart on the down-tilted side of the lot, stuck against the curb, unwilling to pull itself back up the slight elevation to the hotel.

People went around us. Poultry farmers: from those who work full time for someone else and tend to a small side business weekends and evenings; to those who take their ideas out of trade magazines, are the targets of national advertisers, and have places to go. They walk, even if to no good ends, the limit of their perceived open yard. But we were standing still. We were in the way. We made a break that divided crowds, flocks. I stood there looking up at her chin and her long uncaring brown hair waving comfortably in the wind, lashing shoulders that looked like they had never hoisted anything overhead. Around us the other conventioneers scratched the pavement, paying us no attention, checking out the serviceable gizzard stones lying all about, investigating small pieces of the flower bed cover, marveling at the trash small enough to blow through.

I pulled myself up as straight as I could and said, "I'd be glad to help with the luggage. I can take it right in now." And I thought: my wife would be proud. She is always harping that I am too tired to do anything that isn't directly connected to the poultry; too stitched to the repeatable with keeping the business books always clean: as predictable and plodding as a summer rainstorm. My days, for her, are one connected action after another with a constancy that we both have become jealous of. She loves me for who I am, for the regularity I have drummed into our common life; but I can be annoying. I know it. I know at times I drive her to indifference, to lackluster mechanization. I try to do better. I can try to muddle the mold. Maybe I can do better now.

Rio feathered a key from some, until that moment, unknown pocket and correctly hit the lock button so the tail lights of her car flashed, sending me in the right direction. Then she slid to another button and popped the trunk. It did not fly open, but I had seen the tail lights and I had heard the latch release. As I walked ahead I could hear her wiggle behind me: slide, and to the side; slide, and to the side. I could imagine dumbstruck poultry farmers frozen in the lot, watching the long, cool length of her pop and crackle, stiff as chicken wire, with all the hints of serviceability you feel in a fresh spool of the galvanized high grade mesh, one that has just ungently dropped off the truck.

And I walked faster, reaching my right hand already towards the trunk, cautioning myself not to throw the trunk open like I were trying to get a spade out of the locker: but to remember with all my courage to gingerly guide it to rise, to let it settle back on its own suspension. Every poult comes into laying season in its own time. It would do me no good to rush.

I would take my time. I would do right.

The handle on that fine first bag jostled in her trunk stared at me like our most fierce rooster, having knocked down the day and announced his triumph over it. He would sit on the fence looking at me, already up and dressed and bending into the morning's practical drudgery, thinking he had accomplished something, thinking there was something I should acknowledge in his full-throated mastery. Each of us might stand there a second or two, each thinking himself the cock of the yard.

And so I eventually took in two pieces of luggage while she led me off with one and I was thinking of the days I first knew a henhouse, first collected eggs by hand, how I saw wonder in it.

That night for two hours I kept the wife on the phone: she, wondering what there might be about a poultry convention that could so queue my interest; why I would tell her the details of the lobby, the parking lot, the room and its in-tub whirlpool; its small business work desk where an un-idle man might roost comfortably for hours; and the vinyl chair that squeaked against my skin as I slid in and out of it. It was all new to me. And every time she would say in closing we would talk of it when I got back, I would say *I wish you were here*, and begin the long march to the henhouse again.

Deep into that night, I dreamed of the hens of our private stock, the ones we keep close; the ones that supply our personal doldrums of eggs; the ones with which we are comfortable. I eat those eggs almost daily, and I think nothing of it. I don't think at all about those good enough-for-me eggs, and I eat. I enjoy. But to our roosters, a hen is a hen. It works both ways.

I dreamed of the rooster that holds that private part of the yard. Most of my days, that rooster might be the metal contraption that sits atop our decorative, useless weathervane. I see it, I hear it; but I do not see it, I do not hear it.

In my dream, I am strutting just outside the wire: I scratch the dry ground, and my beak thrusts into the thundering heart of the day; I throw back in pure, reactive aggression my resplendent coxcomb; and I screech the blind desire of choice into the sun-stained, dreadfully wakening air. Then, still desperately trying to hold onto sleep, I make the raptor's choice; and I wake sweating and un-feathered into the dark: alone, I believe; alone, and listening for movement in the sheets.

A SEASON OF WANT

He had not been to an auction since his death. He had not been to much of anything, really. Until very recently, it took all of his time to get the hang of operating robotic arms, and of flexing plastijoints, and deftly manipulating an omnigrasp. It takes time as well to understand that, when he felt tired, he might just be standing in a region of shadow and his battery could be too low to make up for what his solar array was missing. And pressure was hard to learn: push open the door, not punch straight through it.

These things take months, but at least he was able to go through the process. Only the very rich can afford not to die. Even the moderately rich do not have the resources to be resurrected as cybercitizens. You have to have your financial fingers into everything. Your funds need to make you indispensable - and, consequently, rich enough to have a life assurance contract that puts you into the nanocarbon and metal housing of your choice, when the time of expiration hits you.

George knew that it would take perhaps years for some of the synaptic connections in his brain to meld properly with the adapting electronic leads. Touch was just not the analysis of pressure points and abrasion. The mind had to rewire itself as well, to come up with the sensation of touch all over again, and bond it to a new type of data stream unabashedly coming in. This took will and science and - why not say it? - talent. It is not for the less gifted.

"I think they are going to come out with the cheap ones in a minute."

Beside him, a squat canister of a machine, one of the old, now frowned on type, extended a stalk eye to look up at the stage, and added to his earlier proposition, "No, it won't be long now."

It took a while to sense speech as speech. At first, it was just a dull thud at the base of what would have been his left big toe - if he were still alive and had toes. But it had come around, and he now could tell this was speech, communication, and not a nail in the foot or a breeze on the back of the neck.

The canister looked over at him. "You know, they always bring out the useless ones first. They build your appreciation. Sometimes I think these first few are not really for sale. They just want to set you up."

George turned his head to eye the speaker with both of his best-in-class eyes. "It's my first auction in a while. I might have lost the full appreciation of how much gamesmanship goes into it."

The canister returned its stalk eye to its socket. "Well, if you are here, you've done some gamesmanship in your time, too. You can't afford one of these," he thumped himself on the side with a telescoping arm, "if you haven't put by a few winnings during your life."

It all gets back to what you can afford. George Fromm, the oxygen salesman, selling oxygen to entire continents and their gasping citizens. What can George afford? George can afford to cheat death. George Fromm, died the first time on October 13, 2117. Died again? No, never again.

George glanced across the crowd and could see that better than two-thirds of them were cybercitizens. Still, a few reeking, heaving biological magnates were in attendance, but their numbers had been dimming for years. One day, soon, they would be rare in anyplace that meaningful business is done.

To the canister he said, "Well, since this is my first time in a while, are there any hints you can give me?"

"Yes. Don't bid against me."

George was pondering whether he wanted to continue this conversation, when the first item came up for bid. It was a man of forty, according to the public information screen behind him. The rest of the item's history flashed below the identifying tag. Accountant. No known health issues. Appendix removed.

No one bid. What would George need with an old accountant? He had an ancillary attachment now that fed the status of his corporate holdings directly into his sub-consciousness. Maybe the old canister would need him, or perhaps one of the still living bidders would feel better with a biological unit keeping his numbers clean. Likely, the canister would be better of just ordering an upgrade. The breath-and-sweat crowd? No one made a move to offer even the listed lowest acceptable bid, and the man was quickly moved off.

The next was a woman close to fifty, with a resume that listed domestic service, and one bad knee. Again, not even the minimum bid. A bad knee on a marginal offering would be enough to kill any deal. George was beginning to think these first items were just a warm up. He had seen the play many times before. Let the bidders get settled, let them get a feel for the auction's geometry, let them scope each other out and see who could be a rival, who might be an ally, who really didn't care about anything but winning.

The crowd had shifted its attention. A biological unit was arguing something with a new model cybercitizen. Two cart venders were hawking something at the far back of the crowd. A surveillance drone went by.

Everyone surely knew the woman was a teaser, a place holder. She was moved off the far end of the stage, soon to act as a filler in yet another auction held later, held elsewhere.

After that came a 2005 Ford Focus. Fairly good condition, with mostly original parts. Just a smattering of synthetics here and there to make it safe to be near. A museum piece. Something to hold a party at the house around. George thought of bidding, but he had no room for it, and he could not even fit in it. A conversation piece, nothing more. A piece of ancient history he might keep with his hundreds of other pieces of ancient history he had collected the last time collecting artifacts of ancient history had been the rage. When something falls out of favor, you have to warehouse it. A lot of bother.

Items came and went, and not until the seventh or eighth item was a bid placed: minimum bid on a length of hand woven Afghan carpet. Not all that useful, but rare ever since Afghanistan was erased. The frill at the carpet's edge could be downright dangerous. The new owner would need to take care when he displayed it. Liability lawsuits can gum up any cozy display of boundless wealth. Properly encased and free from deterioration, the investment might appreciate. Or something even rarer could come onto the market, and the investment stagnate. These sorts of transactions are risky, unless you really want the item. But, in the end, anything someone picks up here gets judged by its investment potential. So, even if you want the rare carpet, what you get is the data track of each day how valuable it is in a volatile market.

George was beginning to wonder why he had come, what his plan had been. The canister was obviously looking for something. Others in the crowd were no doubt waiting for some particular item to come up. Yet others were comparing bargains, looking to play the resale market. What was George looking for? George wondered. He had been adjusting to his own death, and meticulously sorting out the curiously served inputs his new cyberbody was feeding him, and he thought: more. Just as with the will and unsympathetic drive that had made for him his great, unchallengeable wealth, his desire was always for more - even after one death, he was still wanting more. He had left the body behind and come into the rebirth of limitless life and everlasting property rights. But he wanted more. More. He just did not know more of what.

He thought the auction might sort it out, might provide him the stimulus that would match his constitutional insatiability. He was becoming everyday ever more efficient in his afterlife, matching himself to the mechanical, learning to map his old senses and feelings to his new data feeds, inputs and interrupts; but was he becoming ever more effective, ever more happy, ever more complete in accumulation, ever more true to his self-given purpose?

Thirty-seven items into the auction and he was about to leave, when a girl was brought up in offer. She stood there, hands clasped in front of her; her soulless brown hair drifting down over her shoulders and making coy curls at the top of her chest. She kept still, her eyes emptily focused on the front line of the audience: solid. On the screen she was listed as nineteen, no known defects, former lacrosse player, no injuries, bilingual with New English and Spanish, no specialized skills.

George regarded her for a while, and then felt the slightest twinge at the center of his back. Or what his brain thought was his back, as he had had no back ever since his death. But there was this strange sensation. Not an unpleasant sensation. Perhaps even a pleasant sensation. A paste of ignition on a pool of imaginary geometric emotions. One reminiscent of what he would occasionally feel in life during those gleeful years when he had mistresses and secretaries who doubled as mistresses and a number of wives. There had been wonders of women in his life, spattered across his days as only they can be spattered for a seriously wealthy man. Since his death, he had no need of the complement sex. His own sex was just a matter of convenience - he had thought of himself as male in life, so why not continue the idea in death? It does no harm. But it does not matter.

The girl's hands in front of her seemed less submissive than pre-pared, yet the shoulders dipped down a bit and the head tended deferentially forward. Collateral on a loan, perhaps. Her athleticism stood out, and her lines were serious and tight. She must have a pertinent elasticity. There would be thunderstorms in her; though, over time, she might be a steady rain.

George looked over to the canister, who was watching the crowd and not the stage. No doubt, the canister was looking over the reactions of bidders, looking for stooges, for stand-ins, for people who, probably like himself, were here simply to get a fix on the subsidiary markets: to mix, as only a dead citizen can, the probabilities for resale with the intuition of market vagaries. The canister did not have an interest in this offering, nor it seemed did any others in the audience.

A bland biological unit. Born once, like himself, but apparently unable to achieve like he had forced himself to. Placed in auction for one reason or another - debt, or in exchange for sustenance, or as a serial extension on a family's generations deep oxygenation plan. He held the options on many such plans.

George reached inside himself to see if he could draw out the smoky sensation, if he could taste the edge of its fickle electricity. The feeling was becoming ever more familiar to him with each rattling half second weathered. There was some sort of drive in this chemical ledge, some matrix of hot and cold pushing across the same landscape, creating. Begetting. There was the sense, yes, of more. More to gather, more to take, more to withhold, more to enslave, more to own, more to enjoy, more to define, more to simply spring into being out of elements collected. He had to roll this itch about, to place it where it should be, or give it a new home where it could grow and feed and maybe devour. More. Yes, more.

The girl looked slowly and willfully across the whole of the audience, her woman shape imprinting its data pathway on George: bends and folds and stretches and breathing, real breathing. Storms, and a clearing at morning.

George tried to mentally ease the sensation in his long missing back around, to find its connection, to encapsulate it into a unit he could manage, to find for it a description more useful and less illustrative. He felt the quiver almost like sand in true fingers. George edged himself sideways, to block the creeping curious stalk eye of the canister. Just before the intriguing girl was led off - to be kept perhaps as a profitless teaser for the next auction's crowd - George reached forward, ever so elegantly, holding back the sudden stream of his impossible expectations, and trying to fondle with an open register the bizarre and even morbidly welcomed sensation that was growing within his adapting circuitry; and, with perfect pitch and the round O of a chanter's last canticle, depressed for the first time in his afterlife his dizzying bid button.

THE INVESTIGATIVE PROCESS

The post office does not have his address. It is not in any zip code. It is not serviced by any particular post office station. It does not appear in any forwarding list. It is not attached to any special do-not-deliver group. It is not on the list of addresses where the dog runs loose, or where the woman of the address wears wonderfully tight white shorts and has a wiggle that worries and wafts spectral a letter carrier's expectation all along the length of the winding way to her door. It does not lie with the collection of addresses having the most creative mailboxes. It does not sort with all those tired addresses that have a mere slot in the door. To the post office, it simply does not exist.

For a long while, the post office thought that he, himself, might not exist — but there is a web page. And an e-mail address. There must be someone corporeal to move the keys, update the pages, provide ever more scintillating content. In one way or another, he must exist. He must comprise the center of the virtual waves that grow around him. The gravity of his electronic efforts demands his corporeality, while it acts as the shadow of the real being lying behind the digital architecture.

With his existence so proven, then he must have an address. Everyone has an address, even if only a temporary one. The post office simply does not know it.

For a while, the search for his address went sadly dormant. The post office has only so much recourse to investigative resources. If he were involved in mail fraud, then they could hunt him without reserve. If there were some sort of wire fraud, or child pornography, or illegal gambling - and, indeed, there might just well be - the post office could wield its mighty enforcement arm and seek to pry his address from whatever black hole of indemnity it might have run down. But the post office can only guess at such things: it does not know.

One postal worker, however, took it upon himself to intercede. On a single piece of paper he wrote "Please send us your address", and stuffed it into an envelope with simply the address of "Unknown", purchased with is own funds a first class stamp, left no return address penned or stuck on it so that the dodge of returning it to sender would be impossible, and dropped it into a fresh metal letter box. And then the post office could be unending in its action. It has the mail to deliver, customers to serve, a mission to meet. There are no limits to this duty, running all the way back to Benjamin Franklin.

Perhaps he is itinerant. Perhaps he lives at the addresses of other people, moving when he feels in danger of being tied to one particular address. Perhaps he is really an entire movement of people, all with valid addresses - and all the addresses are mixed together, in so large a collection that finding any one and saying definitely it is his, or theirs, is impossible. Perhaps looking for it is like looking for that one camel that, upon the addition of one more straw, will have its back suddenly, and like the collapse of an event horizon, break.

Do not get ahead of me: he did not answer his e-mail. He would not respond to a query on his web page. We traced the Internet provider but could produce no warrant. We tried for a warrant, but, while having no address may be criminal, we could not prove that the post office not knowing the address was the same as not having an address, and so the loophole robbed us of a warrant. And, after all, the Internet provider may not have had an address for him. In any case, we would have to be creative.

More and more elements of the post office are engaged to find this address. Some employees work on it full time. There is thought to designate a special office, a branch with its own address, to do nothing but search for this address. There have been a few internal contests - time off awarded to the worker who can come up with the most novel and likely way to find the address. People who think out of the box are awarded daylight and fresh air. A woman in night sorting came up with the best idea last quarter. I have long forgotten what it was, but she was allowed to take off an entire week — though she spent it inspecting addresses, going around herself to knock on the surely criminal doors of the suspicious ones, comparing the expectation of local lore with the actual outlines of the residents she found.

At the beginning, the lack of an address seemed but an oddity, and a hiccup in the orderly delivery of mail. Then it became a bit more suggestive. Later, it became annoying; and later still perhaps a matter of pique played out against the post office; then, after more time, some sort of malice; and now perhaps some desperate and felonious act. It has grown, much like the movements of a five year old might be funny; and yet at fifteen these same movements become suggestive; and at twenty-five they become wonton and happily dangerous; and at thirty-five, hopeful and willing; and at forty-five, routine; and at fifty-five, inept and practiced and well-worn; and at sixty-five, tragic. All the same family of movements — but the sphere of its circumstances changing, evolving, becoming an otiose child of entropy. So it is with this lack of an address.

I imagine the mystery moves two ways. Without an address, there is wonder about the post office. What is the post office thinking? Does it have mail for him? Will the post office long remember the lack of an address? Will this dull and sounding absence resound at employee picnics, be worthy of an amen corner at any particular station's water cooler?

Oh yes. But this conundrum will be solved. I am going to posit that even though he lacks an address, somewhere he possibly has a wife. A wife who probably does not know her everyday, comfortable and electrically quiet husband has no address. Or there is a girlfriend who believes he is as fully addressable as she, and would be aghast to find otherwise. Let us go there. Let us look to see if she has an address of her own, and then follow the numbers wherever the numbers unwillingly lead.

PERSISTENCE

When she sat down, I was shocked that I could see a difference from her physical state last night to her even more limited corporeal condition this morning. She sat in her frumpy, little, too-old-for-her, short nightgown and leaned forward as she fingered her smart phone, one leg twisted back along the side of the kitchen table chair, one leg extended under the table.

"Fran, it seems to be worse." I had only brought up the subject two weeks ago, though I had been noticing the change for more than a month.

"I don't really notice it. It is only you that goes on about it." She had decided to be difficult this morning, starting out with the defensive its-you-not-me stance. She held her smart phone slightly away from her face, blocking any sight she might have had of me.

I looked her over and what kicked me most was that I could not really tell where the edges of her fingers ended and the clear air around those fingers began. They were not really a blur, but more of an apathetic white-out: an ill-defined set that blended into the unspectacular surroundings. They seemed to disappear, as though a change in electrical phase were thoughtlessly propelling them eerily into unseen dimensions.

Then I noticed her bare feet on the floor and I was not sure where the floor ended and her feet began. Where she became reasonably solid, she seemed almost to grow out of the floor, an extension of the more solid substance: or like a mist drifting from a morning's untroubled lake. The back foot was coyly tensed on her bent toes, and the tension stood marginally out; but the foot flat under the table dipped into an alloy of flesh and tile, the molecules of her being tethered too far apart, one from another, to appear capable of being distinctly her much longer.

Starting a while back, her facial features had been becoming a bit of a blur; but it was much harder to notice, as she still used some make-up and there are natural shades of color shifting combatively in any face, so I had only clues to fix on. And the memory of faces last longer than the more practical memories of the rest of anyone's body.

"We might be able to solve this if we talked it out. Maybe we could come up with a reason."

"E-mail," she said, her fingers already alight on the small device's drop down keyboard, flying like amphetamine laced spiders dancing legends on a hot pan.

I turned back to breakfast, fumbling with splitting our English muffins, wishing I had cut them closer to the toaster so I would not have to walk them half way across the kitchen lain open like a morning catch. It is a small kitchen, but the longer I can face the counter, the less likely I am to say anything. I do not like fighting in the morning. And I was sure to lose this fight.

I have been falling out of her life. Last night, like many before, during our checker of love-making, she had kept her headset on and was running over past texts that had collected during the day. The tablet lay beside her and could be operated with one hand, or picked up and held just over my shoulder, both hands arching around my head to each be assigned search and select utility. Afterwards, she sat aslant in bed, as always, sheet bunched at her waist, allowing me to fondle an unannounced, carelessly dangling breast while she tapped out replies, reviewed videos, evaluated the popularity of today's recommended anonymous posts. I lose interest, but I fondle nonetheless, as I think that to do so is part of the role I am supposed to play. This has been our ritual for months, our compromise; but last night she appeared to notice less than usual that I was, at that time, with her in the room. I have always religiously tried to be no bother - to not disturb her, to not get caught up in any peripheral connected to whatever device at the moment draws in her attention. I look for the wires, wait for the day when the few remaining appliances that are not yet wireless do finally go acrobatically free of physical connection. As though foreplay, I expertly position the two of us so that she can access without much effort whatever device she chooses to work on during my barely perceived pursuit of frenzy. And, once the position is established, I do nothing to obstruct, nothing that might require a movement of the screen, or of us, or which might cause a static in the headset.

Of course, I have wondered: if I were to knock out a cord, or with a misplaced elbow switch off the device, might I get from her an angry buck, or a livid kick, and maybe some life. Fingernails on the back in retribution would still be fingernails on the back.

I have my own devices, but I was never a fan of constant connection. When I met Fran, she was checking her account balances from a corner table in a local wireless hot spot, daintily sipping coffee or tea - I never learned which - while I looked over the engaging length of her. My gaze grew more longing and emboldened by the depth of her electronic conviction. She was a physical potential tethered to a virtual obsession. She was as solid and real as I sometimes still imagine her, and she seemed to be driven by the gravity that was pulling her into her frighteningly fast digital fancies. I imagined us together, our batteries run entirely down. I abandoned my seat and moved to share her table. When I asked if I could take the cheap plastic chair opposite, she waved me in place with but a flick of her exciting wrist. Every movement she made seemed sensual, counter-poised to the limited quickness she played out against her screen and the embedded keyboard. All around us, couples and singles and groups were texting and e-mailing and making small on-line purchases; and in the anonymity I asked her for her handle. She spoke it like spitting out the head of a chicken. I sent her a picture of myself and a vita she could not then know was written by someone else for someone else, and at some point after scanning it all on her device, she looked up.

She seemed to have no concern for the physical; and so, even at the start, I felt I was being allowed to borrow the magnificence of her physicality, though not really being able to engage in the unevenness of a mutual sexual relationship. Nonetheless, at the cold book of our beginning partnership, she would usually put aside her communications connections long enough for us to accomplish our frenetic prayer to the animal. Or my prayer to the animal; to at least the animal remaining - and perhaps withering even then - within me. Once, she even told me that our sex was nearly as good as something she might catch on one of the personal notifications sites. I should have been proud, I have learned. If it is not in a blog, it is not real.

It did not last long.

At first, she began running a simple connection that required only her visual attention on her laptop, and I learned to accommodate my passion so as not to block out her sight of the screen. I could take as much time as I liked, so long as I was done by the end of the program. Then she began reading e-mails in large text, needing a free hand to scroll; and now listening to text messages converted to voice.

I expect that the fading was already well underway when I met her. I have no idea how substantial she might have been five years ago, or even three: she might have shoved the air around her about and clattered thunderously on simple pavements, or bullied the less substantial gravities of other objects. I might have seen it sooner, had I had some experience with the more full-featured and clear-edged being she surely was back then — when the sharpened drop of her lip meant something, and the dip of a shoulder could birth a man's hope. But I did not catch on to the singularity of her disintegration until I had come out of my infatuation with the unknown, and then improbable, process of making our relationship work: of creating an us out of she and I, no matter the shredded angles and unkempt bends tossed into the blinding bucket of disjointed emotions I had to work with.

I've noticed this fading also to be happening to her friends. When we see them out, hunched over a table at a coffee house or a small restaurant - their laptops or tablets laid out and their fingertips surgically excising cherished attention from the offered mundane in their incoming boxes and bins - and inserting the returned lackluster into their outgoing - or even walking unsteady in the street with their smart phones or tablets held mid chest, and headphones completing their isolation. Even in clothes they seem to me to be fading: fading, as though losing more unnoticed atoms to the wind than their bodies can be bothered to replace. They seem to be, as a class, each day drawing thinner and thinner - not in weight, but in mass, in substance, in the ability to be subject to gravity and its elemental cousins. Each day they are more diaphanous. Each day more light seems to go through them, rather than around: fewer and fewer photons are blocked by them altogether. Their once full shadows suffer.

I see no sympathy in these friends when she sits unseen down and texts them across the room, or calls them into a chat session, flashes a picture from our table - next to theirs - where I sit watching her work the keys and personlessly fall into the screen. The world outside the box seems to find a path through them that is unimpeded; and she shares this distinction by socializing new rituals, ones that leave me further and further outside of her notice, no matter the event, no matter the climax, no matter the understanding or simple recognition I seek - or which I seek to bestow.

She pulls her back leg forward to meet the other and I swear I can see the chair legs through her leg as she lets it glide inelegantly and almost forgotten under the chagrin of the table. When her English muffin pops up from the toaster, I will butter it before I set it down in front of her. She would eat it without butter or jam or anything, so long as it can be done in quick commitments of only one hand, and then back to the keys. She is lucky she lives in a house with a man who eats, and who is willing to cook - if badly and only out of a sense of self-preservation. She barely touches what I put out for her, but I only cook my own meals and then add a little on the side to leave available, hoping she will find her way to it. And it is enough.

She runs a momentarily free hand through her hair and I am sure the light of the solid and recklessly mundane kitchen fixture passes through it more today than it did yesterday. Or maybe this morning's light is brighter than yesterday's. The sun may be adding more to what our simple electricity is offering. Maybe with the passage of one day our sun is more rightly centered on our window, streaming in at a more direct and demanding angle.

But I know better. I will soon slide her this capably toasted muffin, and she will eat less than half of it before getting up and going to synchronize her smart phone with her laptop, checking first thing all the feeds that load faster on her top-of-the-line home-based computer than they do on her mobile companions.

I swear, out of pure animal rage I could kick out the chair, throw her face-first over the table and have my will with any part of her; and, so long as she could still work the smart device, she would not care. Actually, I do not think she would notice. But I eat both halves of my muffin, sitting straight in my chair, looking at the dishwater-tinted wisps of her hair left driveling down alongside the dimming outlines of her occupied face. I know a person who once lived there.

Leaving most of her first half of muffin askew in the plate, she rises, still staring into the screen, and begins to plod towards the workroom we have carved out of our living room, where the electronics thrive and scheme. She holds her smart phone chest high and navigates the hallway by bumping once into the wall. The shoulder of her free hand is drooping like a eulogy.

"Fran," I say softly, but she does not hear. I look for her shadow as she begins to escape the sunlight, and I notice that today, with the carpet in the hallway frisky and flattened for action, she has no shadow at all.

Fran, I think. Is that short for Francine or Francis? Or maybe Frankie, or Frangelica? I don't think I ever knew. I don't think I will ever know. Or maybe her name was never Fran at all.

CONTINUITY

I am looking for the right temperature: an effective, narrow band of elevated warmth. Without an invasive procedure, the best I can do is pick up the radiant heat and calculate against normal human individual variances the likelihood that this one is ovulating, or that one is not; that one is two days before prime, that one is two days after.

Given this species' baseline biology, I have about a 30% chance with purely random selection. But, by adding in the ability to check temperature gradients from across the room, with precision down to nearly one thousandth of a degree, I am bound to get lucky.

Percolating in my internal storage is the soup of donated seminal matter, mumbling with the nanotechnology I have created, all polished and refined over the last few months. Each gamete pairs with its micro-engineered brother, mimicking function to function: repeating, each to the other, patterns in bondage that will persist through the violence of growth and replication.

I run a diagnostic on the recently installed delivery apparatus. The flexible, temperature-neutral tube connects securely from the warmed sack to the telescoping metal insertion device. All seals still hold. The pneumatics of propulsion report within expected operating tolerances, and the adjustability to backflow potential ensures delivery to the proper depth for 98% of the projected potential subjects. The three motors at the base of the insertion device I have tested - independently, and together - and I can accomplish so wide a range of entry angles that any necessary accommodation for desired superfluous gymnastics on the part of the subject will not deter the efficacy of the payload delivery.

The telescoping implant device itself I extend beneath the table to its full length, and then stage by stage retract it. I exercise the three motors at its base through their statistically expected range of motion, with the device held at varying degrees of static length. One man at the next table notes my diagnostics; he taps his companion on the shoulder, and they both point to where I sit, each of them shaking in guffaws and chortles and trying to get the attention of the people at the next table. Undeterred, I rub a little graphite from the table's complementary bowl of lubricants on my splendidly designed device, and fully extend the insertion apparatus to transfer the cooling, slick graphite to the collapsing edges, insuring a smooth extension.

Most people in the bar tonight are configured in couples. If I were to try to split the female from one of these committed couples, chances are that the male would object and my intention could be spilled: and for me it would be back to the repair shop, my memory flashed, my added engineering removed and disassembled for scrap, my nanotechnology-enhanced gametes surrendered to some biotech graduate student for spiritual analysis. No. I want to find some lone female with the look of adventure and no fear of novelty, one that would be at first amused by the pluck of an unaccompanied robot, and then astounded at the mission I advance - yes, even intrigued to imagine if I can be all that I say I can be. And yet, a woman who can remain - for the clipped duration of our intimate transaction - unsuspecting of my desire for a lasting, repeatable architecture.

And a woman that is the right temperature.

I drum an omnigrasp on the table and try to look suave. I have no illusions. I am an oddity. Even just in being here, I am an oddity. How many robots have you seen sitting alone at a bar, fingering the free graphite and looking perhaps one shot of lubricant short of a core dump? My small talk is of rumored upgrades, better grades of graphite, the latest rotation couplers, or whether the stray interstices unplanned in holographic memory are actually 'thought'. I do not intersect well with human leisure time and the banter of casual carnality. I am, for most attending biological units, perhaps a memorable moment in a pleasant evening's outing - and then the erstwhile subject in nearby human conversation is on to the dazzling brute with the dazzling streak of yellow in his dazzling brown hair, and the dazzling brace of his trousers sucked in like curtains unable to resist an open window.

But eventually, there will be one woman who wants to know a bit more. I will see her across the room, nursing her drink, and my sensors will grade her omnipresent leaking temperature; I will compare the statistical chance that she is at the right state of ovulation against the statistical chance that, with the establishment's closing time fast approaching, I could possibly find another subject exuding any better of a statistical showing. Availability, temperature, and the location's closing door of opportunity will intersect in a splash of possibility, and a subject will emerge. I hum in system idle mode, alert for the possibility.

I don't expect immediate success. Males and females stumble through this ritual night after night and even when both are desperately hoping for success, there is often no success. They dance and shimmy around their intentions and spit out avatars in the likenesses they think most palatable. I do not have the programming for such guile and threadbare acting. I can only do so much before my logic circuits clamp shut. It may take me a few nights to get the method down right, and I have the disadvantage - or the advantage, if I can play it - of not being a member of this circuitous species. I have to embellish my purposes and elaborate my existential circumstance against whatever collection of prejudices and proclivities I perceive in my intended subject. I catalog, I learn. I have storage to spare. I recharge during the day, and have the battery power to remain persistent each night. Play the right angles, properly gauge the potential subject's propensity for novelty, learn from each rejection, and I will eventually succeed. I am mechanical: I have the will to try, try, try again.

The more nights I am seen in this place, the more likely I am to be accepted as an alternative to one of the habitual males that linger hopelessly about hoping to use the net of alcohol and boredom to ensnare a stray mate for the evening. I turn on my sober charm. I chat up my mechanical advantages. I spin the opportunities in my uniqueness. I offer to provide more decimal places of pi than anyone living in this establishment could possibly recall.

But I do not hint that I am looking for the mother of my child.

The raven haired, matronly model at the nearest end of the bar has just lost her bid on a man who I have seen here before do better. I catch the corner of her eye, and nod, one multi-joint antenna tipped seductively in her direction. I spin the motors on my insertion apparatus and test the extension potential one more time, raising slightly the table. Surely, she thinks my knee has brushed the table's underside and sent it a-kilter with my momentary loss of attention. What else could she suspect?

I settle the table with an arm and she slides off her bar stool, dropping her chin to look at me through the tops of her eyes; and I can see from this angle that her seriously constructed hips would suit my intended industry just fine. Space enough. Her heart could beat for two as long as it needed to. Her bone structure could support the weight of cybernetics evolving. With every slow twist of her high-heeled walk, my seduction subroutines are swapping from the cache into core.

Just let me get her temperature.

THE JOY OF LIVING TO TWO HUNDRED

There are a lot of bad things that come with being two hundred years old. The worst right now is the sex.

Of course, surviving all the way to two hundred means, at the happy least, that you are not yet dead. And it makes for celebrity. The next oldest man is one hundred fifteen; he lives in a nursing facility, isn't quite sure who he is, and sleeps most of the time. He hasn't groped a nurse in twenty years. His birthday party is a big affair for everyone, except him.

I do relatively well. I live with my publicist; I get around by myself; I still enjoy some foods, though most things of late taste like oatmeal. I dress myself. When going short distances, I don't even use my cane. Short, of course, is a relative term.

I remember faces that I don't like, and faces that I do like. Those in between I have been regularly forgetting all of my life, so what is the loss now?

I did not think sex would be a problem. Like most men, I thought I would have more sex from the ages of sixteen to twenty-five than I would have in all the rest of my life, combined: casual sex, dating sex, purchased sex, group sex, married sex, cheating sex, blind sex, angry sex, hot-line sex, anonymous sex, internet sex, sex when I was fashionably alone. To tell the truth, I was not all that upset when my great personal oceans of sex began to dry up, and the engine on my boat started to sputter and occasionally softly shoot only smoke.

Okay: up until one hundred I would pay some blonde - a willing veteran with the work experience to focus on the cash and not on the condition; some peach blonde, with her hair coloring a month past the need for a bathroom sink retouch; some well-worn, busted odometer peach blonde - for the semblance of a blow job just so I could tell myself that, oh boy, for nearly six seconds I had two-thirds of an erection. And even up to a few decades ago I would slip into bed with one of my wrinkled, desiccating, casual, remotely once female, friends - who would be themselves only a month or so from that last trip to the nursing home or the funeral parlor - and roll about, the two of us clumsily imagining ourselves as having a bull-flaccid, torrid fling.

Then, for nearly seventy years: nothing. Nothing at all. I would look down in the shower at my withered testicles dangling lower than their lack of weight gave them any right to; and regard my pecker - which was never any great slayer - recoiled into a flat tire shape and looking like it were afraid to peer out of its squashed, cushioning folds of skin. I would try mental exercises to see if I could generate a quiver of stiffening - not expecting any sort of coming out party, or even the shadow of the monster trying to poke briefly into the light. No, nothing so grand. Just a tingle that would say: *I'm listening, I'm trying.* I would not try long. I was resigned.

I was living alone in my trailer back when I was one hundred ninety-nine and about to slip headlong into the machinery of having year two hundred behind me, when I got a call from some newspaper and a lady asked if she could come by to interview me.

"What for?" I asked. I'm generally successful at not being worth anyone's time.

"Why," she said, "you are about to become two hundred. No one else has ever been documented past one hundred twenty two; and even the rumored, undocumented, oldest people are less than one hundred sixty. You are a legend, and a medical marvel. All the world should know about you." She sounded like she believed it. I had no reason to think ill of the lady, but I would have bet then that she was good at sounding like she believed all sorts of things.

"Well," I said, "so long as I can tape my reruns, why not come over and I will tell you whatever I can remember. When you are one hundred ninety-nine, and sniffing over the edge at two hundred, reruns on the tube are pretty damned important."

She knocked on the door later that afternoon and I hollered for her to come on in. Being open to invaders is much easier than having to get up to unlock the door, so the door had been unlocked for almost thirty years.

She was a pert little thing. I have no idea what age. Back then, women between fifteen and sixty all pretty much looked alike. Given my recent experiences, I've gotten women sorted out now into under twenty, twenty to fifty, and over fifty; though plenty of times younger women get into that center group, and older women drop into it as well. It can't be helped.

She sat down on my seldom used couch, in a mid-length tight little skirt and a plain button blouse and proceeded to ask a number of questions I would have forgotten even without later excitement, her conversation laced with praise for me getting to one hundred ninety-nine, as though it were some race and I had put out a better strategy than the other runners and so merited this great victory. Okay, so I had not been hit by a bus, killed by a jealous husband, or got the wrong bug up my bum at a public toilet. I guess being lucky deserves a lot of credit.

At the end of it, she put away her notebook and asked me about sex. Taking the question at face value, I said, "Why, yes, I do remember it, at least in general terms."

She shook her head just slightly. "No, no, I mean do you still have sex?"

Thinking a bit more on the subject, I said after a while, "Well, I think it is still there. Half the time when I take a whiz I dribble all over my balls, but the main whacker seems to be down there, even if it spends its days hiding."

"No, no," she said, "I mean do you have sex, make love, partici-pate in sex play?"

My ears don't always clean out so well. I would say that comes with age, but, actually, I've had that affliction all of my life. Tried everything to get the excess wax out, at least until I found a good side to losing the trailing ends of most conversations. I said, "What?"

And she said, "How would you have sex with me?"

I thought: unsuccessfully. I had images of wheezing and commanding the old Thunder Stick to rise up and deliver. I could see myself passing out as the blood looked down at my loins and said I'm coming, but don't wait for me. I saw myself with a hip broken beyond any replacement or repair. In my imagination, I thought - and then I thought no, not in my imagination: I'd make up too many new steps and forget others and get my memories all twisted around and wore out, ending with a headache, maybe a stroke, and forgetting my reruns.

But what I said was, "Any way you want it, sister!" And she stood up and reached around to unzip the back of her skirt and somewhere in the process my pants got onto the floor and her under-things ended up on the couch and in a magically strange way in that rerun-wrecking hour I think I might have had an erection. Not much of one, mind you, but maybe an inch, perhaps even a glorious two stallion inches, pushing out to see what all the uncommon ruckus was.

She did all the work, and she was a marvelously gentle woman. Agile, too. She had to be. At one hundred ninety-nine, I was as fragile as a child's tinker toy figurine. And I had done nothing like this in seventy years. More if you count the blow jobs and torrid wrestling as simple erotic exercises intended to scare off the demons of emasculation. Here, she was working an architecturally sound sex. Not that I had an orgasm, or that anything shot or even dribbled out of my stunned and amnesia-lulled member. Not that she was howling in climax at any point, or so physically wracked that she crushed my pelvis or fractured my hip or nipped the bones of either arm or either leg, or overturned my chair, or clawed my back with fingernails suddenly grown into talons. No, she was methodical. No whimsy here: she had a plan.

And she was successful, I could see. Not that she had accomplished a wonderful, lets-do-this-every-Tuesday, sex; but that she had had sex, or what both of us, to the fraying ends of our life-long honor, would claim forever was sex, with a man who had reached one hundred ninety-nine. In fact, she had had sex with the oldest man in the world. How many people have done that?

Somewhere, surely - out there somewhere - some one hundred six year old guy was dry humping a drunken, passed out nurse, thinking he was the oldest man ever to get into the shallow part of that woefully tight pool - all for nothing. He could stop right where he was, save his energy, take a rest, stop mentally embellishing every long past romp on the kitchen table he had ever had or wished he had had, and blessedly go back to his reruns. It was over. I and this reporter held the record. Take that, mister dry and mistress drunk. Done and done.

I was surprised that I was able to dress myself, and even that I watched her dress with some sense of satisfaction and appreciation. I even stood, and walked her to my door, watching her wiggle down the rotting steps that only then I thought about having replaced. Maybe with a set built with two-by-sixes. Maybe pressure treated and nailed not simply like a box bisected, but instead with a center brace and flashing where the top step reached the ledge of the trailer. Maybe a concrete retainer at the base so the steps would not tip if you balanced too far forward, or too far back, or too far left, or too far right. I could get that guy Duncan, two trailers over, to do it. He worked cheap.

I did not think about the rerun until near bed time, which of late has been dusk. I checked my old style tape machine and, sure enough, it had run to the end, but it had my rerun on it at the start. So the day was a success from all angles. I had a victory beer, sat up fifteen minutes later than I should, and slept like the dead.

Three days went by and I was getting back to routine when some-one knocked and asked to come in and I hollered that it was open and in walked another woman, this one in a pair of shorts and a t-shirt. I asked, "What can I do for you?" while she stood there and let the light she had let in with the open door lap around her and get to the work of making shadows.

She tilted her perniciously pouting little mouth and said, "Well, I work with Betty."

Names. My own I have stitched into my clothing. Not so I can claim the clothes when I get separated from them. No. So I can remember my name. "Who is Betty?"

And she put a hand on her hip, cocked her whole left side so far out of joint it would have torn me in half had I tried it, and said, "Betty, the one who was here three days ago to get your story."

So her name had been Betty. At least I thought that was what this new girl said. "Oh, yes, I remember. Betty. What can I do for you?"

I was thinking of a cartoon. She reminded me of someone in a cartoon. Couldn't remember who, but it was in a cartoon. And she said, "I want to ask you something."

One of those cartoons made for adults back when cartoons were wedged into the movies between features, and then years later were trucked out for kids when they invented television. And I said, "I ain't getting any younger, so you had better go ahead and ask."

There, she straightened herself back into upright and flop, off came those shorts, and with the light still wiggling in from the open trailer door, I was staring right at the fact that for her, the carpet didn't match the drapes.

This one was much more aggressive than Betty, or whatever her name was, had been. I thought a couple of times I might get injured. But this was twice in one week and I figured heck, for one hundred ninety-nine, it would be worth it. And, even more, there was an edge to her drive that seemed to kick some hormone or another lost drowsily in my rusting body into wearily raising its head, as old Thunder Stick actually poked out I bet a full three inches this time and I could feel I was actually fishing some brush infested top waters, if only for three or four seconds. But fishing is fishing, and I was going to put this notch on the wall. Matter of fact, I had not notched the wall for Betty, or whatever her name was, but I would do so as soon as I got myself out of the current affair and my energy had come back from its nap in the kitchen.

So now there were two women in the world who had had sex with the world's oldest man. Live long enough, and you will see wonders you could never have imagined.

Two days later, the third did not go so well. But I don't think she minded. She went off with half her clothes back on and half in her purse and a smile the size of all the cheese in Wisconsin and maybe some from Vermont, too; and I got to thinking I was never going to get those steps fixed, and had no need to. People got up them, people got down them. Those steps must have been there better than twenty years:

slowly, cautiously rotting. Duncan was not going to get a day's wages out of me for fixing something that works perfectly well.

So there were three women in the world who had had sex, so to speak, with the world's oldest man. I hope it made them happy. Myself, I liked it well enough. I've seen most of my reruns eight or ten times, and I was beginning to remember parts of them. And I had made those women feel better about themselves. Each had left my trailer like they were brand new. I could still wow the ladies.

I knew what was going on. Ladies four and five did not even pretend to be connected to the first and her newspaper report. A newspaper report I never saw, by the way. But I don't read the papers. I know everybody wants to be somebody. Being yourself seems just too hard. You can make a bigger splash if you have a better angle. Wow, you had sex with the world's oldest man? What was it like? Did he climb on top? How long did it take him? Did it feel any different than it does with a normal man? Not many ladies can say they have turned socks and stockings with a man who has gotten to one hundred ninety-nine. Did you have to do like they say: treat him like an antique car, get him started by hand, and then jump on before he craps out? You did not hurt him, did you? You must feel really lucky. That is so special.

Normal man. A normal man.

So I got a publicist. You cannot advertise these things, but there are ways to put the word out. I moved into his place so he could keep my schedule. At my age, keeping a schedule is what I live for. Expectation calls your mind away from what you are really expecting. When my birthday came about, we made a big public affair of it. Two hundred and still counting! I don't remember the faces of the people who came to the party.

Each lady who shows up thinks she is one of the brilliant few to push out this sinfully simple plan. This is her wickedly special idea. This is where she is going to stand out from the crowd. Her moment. Or my moment. One or the other. I greet them at the door, usually clad in my carpenter's sleeveless t-shirt and a pair of boxers. I get them over to the couch where I can ask them to carefully bend precipitously over the back. That way I do not have to distinguish one from the other. They all look pretty much the same, from that angle. Especially with my glasses off. I can focus on me, I can focus on hitting the target, I can focus on challenging myself to interrupt their often giddy, ridiculous giggling with some real intent. I lean into them as hard as I can, even if I cannot penetrate. I do not believe any of them have a thought that real sex might happen, that I might be able to slip a little way into their species survival port and let go my hope for new sons and daughters, firing my intent like the stale air from a corpse. And for nearly all there is no real sex: just a rubbing and a grinding, and some women in courtesy backing away from the couch and handing me my dropped boxers afterwards; and then I shuffling, weary and worked and worn, off for a nap. And for the few I can actually know the inside of, there is a stop to the laughter and a hang fire while they wait to see if there is more and more there never is, not even dry smoke joyfully imagining it is an invading lightning rammed home from the reborn Thunder Stick.

Each gets a signed picture.

I am thinking of going into franchise. I can set up shops around the country, each manned by a much younger man. It would be an open secret that, obviously, I could not work so many store fronts. My face would be pasted on each door, and each woman would be given a signed, frame-worthy picture of me afterwards: a winsomely crooked smile inhabiting my lips and leading each to wonder what scurrilous hedonism I might be thinking. An imposter would meet the customer in a darkened room - someone an eighth my age, perhaps, but affecting my stoop and dragging along at my accustomed pace and doing very much to put on a thin show of being me. The couple could screw or not, but the woman would leave with my picture, and with a tale of how she is one of the few women in the world to have had sex with a two hundred year old man, even if the fellow she had sex with looked to be twenty-five and was as hard as a stainless steel vibrator. Or not. That is not the part of the transaction that matters.

I wouldn't charge much.

Each woman could still imagine, by going through the motions, that she was among only a handful of lucky platforms, even as the precious thousands grew ever more numerous. I might travel, and stop unexpectedly at a few locations to slip in a working appearance with some randomly ennobled customer. Only she would know she was getting the authentic treatment. I would putter away a few seconds with Miss Anonymous and she would not only be paying to be special, but would actually in this case be special. And if I get into one of my coughing fits mid-effort, she might have some real fun out of the adventure.

It could make all this work and bother and schedule-slaying worth it. I could make a name for myself, and for a host of others. All the mathematics and none of the excitement. But it could work for me. A man needs a purpose when he is looking at the short end of oblivion. And the money: I could leave what my publicist doesn't skim to my children.

TAKING CHARGE

What is it that you wanted? I'm still stocking the canned salmon, so this protein won't be ready for detailing for another hour. Until then you can sashay over to the mutton and count ligaments to your heart's content. Really. No one minds at all. I don't see how you can stand in those heels, and all the young boys at the ends of mother's arms will be measuring how long those lover-crusher legs are: but go ahead. The mutton is really unforgiving. You should go look at it.

After you've gone, your sex hangs in the air like a winter's widowed full moon. There are no small spots of it, no ethereal mists: just one huge distraction hoisted like pterodactyl teeth barely out of reach. A body does not have to be here to sense it. People come in, stand dumbfounded for a minute, look around as though somewhere there should be a surprise. Maybe the surprise is at the end of this aisle; maybe in the drop ceiling. Maybe the man stacking salmon is a serial killer. I don't know what it is, but it is something and it is boundlessly disturbing: but in a sweet, cherry cigar smoke sort of way. I say: go check out the mutton.

I remember the first time I put my arm around a woman's waist. She was a girl, actually. The frightening thing is that the sensation I noted most at the time was how crisp her shirt was. She wore a pair of stiff, noncommittal jeans and a fresh button front shirt and that shirt was as crisp as hand crushed onion paper: a sympathetic crackle and a wise coarseness. It took me a while to be aware of the body beneath the scandalous fabric: that flesh-baiting, deep water concoction that I wanted to dive into and swim through and explore like the underside of a criminal's living room furniture. That shirt was a clown-praise wonder all on its own.

This sedition feels much like that one time enchantment.

In an hour the salmon will be stocked and you will be back and the goldfish and I will be waiting, watching every bit of you as you manipulate your threadbare, one-liner way along the aisle. I won't want to, but I will go painfully erect and you will notice my evolutionary interest, since the pants I wear are really cheap pants: the type of pants that are bought in bulk for unimaginative, uncounted shelving clerks. I guess they don't know that, just like executives, we get silly, unimaginative erections, too.

But I am not going home with you. With me, it is just the canned salmon and all the tales I can tell about mackerel and sharks and how no one can be afraid living secluded in a goldfish bowl. The world ends just over there and just over there and again over there when you live in a goldfish bowl and there can be nothing in it to fear, only the external blacklisted stimuli that I, from the outside, control. And I would never do anything to harm a fellow goldfish.

I have it figured out. You will sashay only half way down the aisle, a jumble of color and dangerous motion and battered breath and a box full of open source abilities, and ask me to reach the last can of salmon I have just stacked: to drop it in your basket. Your sour-soul kind is always doing something like that: disturbing the paroled quiet, playing pattern against pattern. Unraveling. Unraveling every manufactured thing. I have an ocean of a mind that is all my own. I am not reaction alone, sympathetic push to sympathetic pull. I have my own crease in this binary universe. It's all wet, dry, wet, dry, and I stack. You do not have your sea legs yet; and, I swear, you geometry of necessary oneness, you won't unravel me.

THE POVERTY TOURS

Allison did not want one of the standard tours - one of those that simply whisked you out into the populace for a day and then back: nothing left by day's end except the smell of listless light wrestling with grime and animated soot; with perhaps the sting of a small child's cry left in the crook of one's elbow. No. She wanted the full tour, the in-your-face experience, the exposure that would leave a person rubbing unconsciously the insides of her thigh for days, chewing her food ever harder as any meal wore on: a tour that had real edges, and a voice that scolded. Hardship. Disease. Hunger. Privation. All the things that separate a them from an us.

She could have taken one near home, but instead chose to fly to one of those countries with a name the spelling of which nearly everyone had to look up, if they recognized the name at all. A flat land with no coasts and fields as dry as the breasts of a septuagenarian, where the rivers back up and when they flow will do so only violently. The airport was like any airport, modeled in a style that would appeal to those with the money to fly, made to look like it processed people instead of profit, made to look worried with comfort rather than fuel costs, made to look as though no one died in its construction.

Her hotel was in the arc of life just around the air park - a ring one or two sets of buildings deep, with the air concourse at the center as a bulls eye, and harboring all the accommodations air travelers need, including a series of tourist and business and smuggler services. Many visitors never get much beyond these sanitized rings, and souvenir shops wait in the lobbies of all the hotels and are piled in the exit corners of restaurants and on the bottom shelves of convenience stores, and tall prostitutes fortified with ample food and western clothing lean outside of the bars one street back and speak a language made up of a dozen languages all with the same limping prayers and unhinged oaths.

These were all places where one could feel better, but she wanted to feel good.

So she booked a tour from the concierge. Not one of the standard tours that ran two miles inland, paraded the tourist through a village knocked up just to fit the tourist trade, loaded with professional beggars and a fresh crew of starving children every morning and a howling miasma of painted child prostitutes and old men selling charms made out of their former wives' pelvis bones. No, she wanted to get past the tourist ring and into the real countryside, where people were made of uneven angles and held disharmonies without corruption and true victims of chance might starve in front of her; and children would kill each other for the opportunity to steal the contents of her backpack and the guides did not carry guns to give her the false impression of danger, but to make for themselves a safe exit if they had to surrender her to the needing mob and give up the tip they were expecting she would triumphantly leave, just to make it home to their wives in the apartment block made of the dung these people harvest from their stringy livestock and sell to in-town builders as quality brick. The hair at the back of her neck would stand up at the idea of seeing the real thing, the real state of this world, and feeling the wonderful rush of knowing it was a different world than hers. The feel of fresh linen is never so good as just after you have watched someone sleep on dirt because there is not enough straw. Her fingers ever since her decision to take the tour had been alive like hyper-sexed spiders, and could be nothing but playful all through breakfast and even later eagerly skinned the biting light of the lobby while she waited for the bus.

While most tourists would simply go to the sham village, and were loading in their migratory numbers at the primary bus stand, there were two others who were apparently coming with her. The two men seemed to be traveling companions and had the soiled look of experience. She felt better about the tour she had booked, seeing that these two were going with the same firm. She was sure they had done this before. Each had dressed as if they knew what to expect, with long sleeved shirts and full pants - inner shirt tucked in, outer shirt left out - and ankle boots with corded laces pulled out of harms reach: the sign of experienced, thoughtful, well-worn travelers. They sat near her, in the section of the lobby that had been by the concierge designated as the waiting area for this particular tour company.

"You've not been on one of the tours before, eh?" The youngest of the two addressed her, leaning a bit forward, though still far enough away in his leather chair to not appear to be entering a conspiracy. His shoulders dipped forward over his knees and his hands sought each other's company.

"Why, no. Does it show so well?" She would be with these two men for perhaps a day and a half, perhaps two. Both appeared serviceably assembled, without extraneous parts. To be touring with them was not so bad a prospect, if they could get along from the start.

"Not so much. You seem almost prepared, but did you bring any other shoes?" He pointed down at her running shoes.

She thought canvass would be best for the heat, and the soles were thick enough from most stubble. The toe curled up a little and would balance her forward. She had assumed there would be some walking. The road would surely come up to the edge of the village, but the road frontage would be taken up by the more commercial cases, the stronger bodies jostling out the weaker ones, and to see what she wanted to see, she would have to walk into the place, wind her way past the sham and show to get into the real muck and malaise. To get to the real wreckage she would have to muscle past the window dressing.

"I'm thinking I can make good time with these. I took them out for half a dozen running sessions on the track back home to make sure they were broken in." She slipped her foot onto the side, so the tread could be seen by the concerned fellow tourist.

"Yes, but you might find more in these villages to do than stay light on your feet." He leaned back, resettling his shoulders, making himself look wider. " I knocked down a fence post last trip, straight on, and I'm glad I had a set of hard toed shoes. These places look ramshackle, but you would be surprised how hard sticks and thatch, animal hide and bone can be. Henry there had to put a heel on some blighter's forehead just to get past him to see where a kid had drowned in the village latrine. They might look spindly, but anyone's skull can ring right through a flimsy set of shoes."

Henry smiled and brought his size eleven footwear from flat on the floor to up on the balls of his feet, the new boots solid stem to stern, and the laces tucked out of the way. He had an oddly alluring shock of blonde hair that fell playfully out from his ball cap and made just the hint of a question mark on his brow.

Yes, these two could be good touring companions.

She glanced a minute at each of her shoes, rolling them side to side. "Well, don't let the bus leave without me. I'll pop round to my room and see if I've got something a bit more durable." She did have those ankle boots. They had a bit of a short heel and might get uncomfortable, but were solid enough. And they might make for a better look if she was to spend time with these two emergently interesting unencumbered men.

She pushed herself out of the deep leather chair, the cushion slowly rising back into place, silently reclaiming its air. "Remember, hold the bus. I don't want to have to hunt you down", she said as she turned to glide to the elevator. She let her head loll slowly over her shoulder, turning slower than her body, a slight of seductive tension drawn across her midsection. She was hoping the two new companions were watching the sizzle of her fishhook sway as she exaggerated it just barely while she wound her way away and towards the polished gleam of the unopened lift door. After the tour, they would all be in a rush of self-satisfaction, and just the thing to finish the experience off electrically might be to have one of them, fresh from the exult of poverty and ruin and bones and disease, knock on her room door with the bravura of someone who has means. Or perhaps both of them: each knocking separately on the door in thrilling stereo, drilling in time with one hand while griping hard by the neck a negotiated bottle of champagne with the other. Two hands or four, then six, and three glasses for two bottles. The bed was king-sized, after all.

THE REPLACEMENT HUSBAND

I could have had him made with a synthetic skin that reeks a constant temperature, that adjusts to pressure, that could be washed with soap and water. He does not care, but it would be physically easier on me, and more comfortable for the neighbors. At a distance, he would blend in.

Distance I do not care about.

What I see is him, sitting across our living room, with the light playing hide and seek in the metal and synthetics of his exposed joints. His factory standard gray exterior I have polished to brilliance, so that at times he seems a gleam - bulk light finding no place to grab on and in frustration shooting back in all directions, sick at being cast away by him. But at those open joints, the light can squirm in and make little joys of refraction, and I shudder to see it so happy.

On a whim, now and again, I have him wear lounge pants and a shirt. I do not think he believes this mean of me, though in ways it is. With his advanced programming, he understands. He does not notice how comical he is sitting there, an oversized shirt and flannel ankle length pull-overs, perhaps house slippers, executing his idle conversation routine or academically noting the peaks and valleys in kitchen economics.

I keep him well covered in graphite solution, plug him in for regular diagnostics. I take him in when notified of hardware upgrades, and endure the stares of unthinking clerks who have never seen a replacement husband uncovered, left calibrated as bare metal. For them, I kiss him where lips should be, and wait with a practiced look of anxiety as an appliance is removed and another added, or a new chip set - in the back room, where I cannot see or go - is drilled into place.

Later, back home and with any upgrades blandly tested, I will fill his reservoir of synthetic semen and nanites that is consistently his response to sex. That night, he will telescope his cold injection device cautiously into me and execute an unremarkable program that, millimeter by millimeter and half angle by whole, reacts to my vital signs and thrashing body maneuvers, to my temperatures - internal and external - and even the scents of execution and release. At the mathematically prudent moment, he will release an amount of fluid projected to meet my need in this accomplished instant and fill the hollow that has been mine these long years of widowhood.

Then, as after every such event, I will reach over as he lies there between instruction strings, and tap with my tapered nails on his exposed metal shoulder: drumming mechanically out a childhood dirge, which dotted melody he has researched before to be a macabre, unfathomable, spectral warning. It's ringing reminds me of ways in and ways out of my unmechanical despair.

I punish very well.

COMPETITION

You thought this was going to be impossible. You thought it would be nothing but the sound of nails collecting on the ground, a hammer flung at a wall. It might have seemed that way, but when you factor in the amount of determination I can muster, it becomes a simple task. I have the perseverance to be inept long enough to learn to be adept.

Left wing, steady the nail. Right wing, bring down the hammer. Maybe I don't drive them as straight as the farmer might. Maybe I can't drive them flush to the wall. But my nailing will hold two boards together. And that is all I need.

I am not looking for an entry into Architectural Digest. I am just building a coop: my own chicken coop: a place where I can collect my chickens, distinct from the farmer's chickens. I will build the walls and the floor as separate pieces. I'll fashion independently a shelf where the nests will be laid out in a row. I'll string a two-by-four for a perch last of all. At the end, I will pull it together as one modular construction. No castle: a coop.

Sure, the farmer's coop will have straighter lines. It will have lighting and heat lamps and a flap on the door. The roost will be round, fashioned of soft wood. He has money to invest. He has a history of poultry farming. He has done this since he was a distraction as his father was doing this. He has agile hands, and every tool in his shed has a familiar smell to him.

I am not trying to compete. But, as a rooster, I expect some credit for building my own coop, for seeing the market and having determination. And the most select and fattest of chickens will migrate to my coop not because it is warm or angular or stylish or comfortable - but because a rooster built it. Because here they can lay eggs and understand it is not the farmer's rough hands that will pull out the still warm commodity, but the rooster's capitalist clutch that will be seductively stealing along their bottoms, drawing out the means to a profit.

Don't get me wrong. I will construct this first one. But when the profits from this rooster-managed eggworks reach an adequate level, I will farm the menial work out. I will bring in artisans and laborers: local boys who will, at first, have no wish to work for a rooster - until they see that that the color in my money is consistent with the color in the farmer's money; that it slips as well into the dancers' g-strings; that it will draw a six pack of beer as easily out of the convenience store; that it can be placed down in card games as deftly as yesterday's I.O.U.

I can envision rows and rows of coops, with happy chickens depositing eggs at perhaps twice, maybe triple, the pace they would at the farmer's place. Climate control, special feed - none of it will out produce the knowledge of keeping production and profit all in the same species. Out of pride and loyalty our staff will fill our cartons with a ferocity the farmer could never enforce in his lackluster stock.

Over time, ever more of the farmer's chickens will see what a good thing we have going here, and under his fence they will slip, milling at first at the edge of our flock, slowly letting the stink of cottage farming ease off of their feathers and beaks — and then volunteering for the production line. We will have so many prize layers that there will not be a place for everyone. Some less productive employees will be pushed off the end of the line, replaced by the newcomers sneaking in.

What to do? You can't invest this much time and effort into something and have it sucked insolvent like bad welfare. At the other end of the compound, a small, thick walled shack will be built, just by the gate, where a fleet of in-town refrigerated trucks can pull in late at night, slip quietly out without having to travel near where most of the laying is done.

Chicken quarters; chicken thighs; chicken necks.

And now I have three boards nailed to the cross member. All around me the flock is stealing quick glances, surveying the rewarding confabulation as I drop the next board in place to be nailed. They look to me, look back to find gizzard stones, look down to see if the farmer has left his paucity of feed. With the full arch of their legs they are scratching excitedly in the collected dust: *What is it? What is it?*

HOME

As the middle class of the twentieth century gleefully turns itself into the peasantry of the twenty-first, I am sitting outside of the one bank building in town, on a public bench, waiting for the streetlight to turn. I have seen only two cars pass through the intersection, but this light changes with a blistering regularity. The town could not afford to put in a light with sensors, and for my purposes this one is just fine. I see it go yellow, shut my eyes and try to count internally how long it will remain yellow, then try to open myself into sight just as the flicker of yellow goes stammering into red.

The length of the red time is different, and I try to meter that continent, too. The green I am not going to attempt until I get the other two cycles nailed flat.

This is what I do most days for at least two or three hours. After a good rain, I skip the stoplight and move uptown to where the stream runs under our main street, continues down the hill to our river not more than four hundred yards off. After a good rain, the stream is consumed with being different from the stream it would have been without a good rain, and I can see things in its character that those who watch less closely would miss, or perhaps might assign to pure natural fickleness. When both of the banks and the water are together eerily angry, the watching is best.

I do lunch at the hot plate in my one room apartment above the local tourist trap - the Magic Emporium. It sells trinkets and charms and odd rock formations to people puttering about town for the weekend. The owner does well enough that he does not live in the room above the shop. This room would be comically wasted in storage if I did not rent it. It takes a gash out of my social security check, but I have to put myself someplace.

I eat lunch over the hot plate; but for dinner, I dine over the hot plate. Forty-three years in the post-union world stacking another man's profit margin at the brewery two blocks up, and I don't even get the occasional free beer. I would still be stacking and counting beloved cases if the brewery had not been abandoned in favor of the sensuous magic of leveraged financial instruments. Those great evolutionary things I cannot figure out; but they have the job I was dimwittedly resigned to work until I dropped, happily complaining all the way.

I have gotten to where I can catch just a wink of yellow and then the full blare of red. It makes me feel, in a backpack sort of way, useful. I cannot be a consumer anymore: the government check is just too small. I cannot produce: this body is meant to lift and stack and mark progress on a clipboard, and somehow the very drinkable beer I blessed with my productivity got drained dry by insurance on real estate outcomes. Not a producer; not a consumer. Instead, I count light cycles; I applaud the stream in its rock bed seeming after each rain, or after each day, casually different; I try to make up odd jobs. I figure God sees me doing this, whether he wants to or not: I figure that I have in His scheme some utility, if only as a witheringly small part of His own job, a soul that He is by divine contract forced to keep track of. I have my triumphs.

Later I will buy a loaf of bread and two bananas. It will be a highlight. I admit I like the feel of being, just for a moment, a part of the economic parade going by; but then I step out of that calming civic stream and wash up, again flotsam, with my plastic bag of less than extravagant sustenance in my room: with my hot plate and the two half packages of chicken dogs I have left from yesterday in the desk top refrigerator that I hope is still working.

Don't think too long on it. Events come down to necessity soon enough, and location is a state of mind. I take care of myself pretty well, given the lack of care.

Don't worry, it is not your fault. Fault is not a part of it. This is simply where you, too, are going.

THE CALL TO ACTION

I lost my legs when the railroad came through my living room. I was sitting there watching television when the foreman ran in, set up a few cute surveying instruments, sighted along my foyer wall, and called in the crew that laid out the tracks. A few hard clangs and a rattle of steel spiked into my carpet, and there went my legs. Two feet more and they would have had to run the line right through my chest.

As it was, I sat there nearly two hours considering my stumps, until a nice man with both a clipboard and a cell phone told me I had to be moved, as the trial hand car would be through at any time, and there would not be enough clearance if I were still in my seat. Two well fed men picked me up and asked where I wanted to go and out of a lack of imagination I asked them to take me to Mike's next door. Mike and I had planned to watch the Ravens game together that afternoon: I would simply be a bit early.

When we got to Mike's, I realized I had not told my wife I was going to Mike's early, so I borrowed Mike's phone and called.

"Honey, I went to Mike's early. The railroad put in new tracks and I was in the way. With the installation, they cut off my legs."

"Oh, and how long ago was that?" I could feel her prop one hand on her hip and cock her head back. You cannot live with a woman as long as I have lived with her and not predict her body position from the mix of music and noise in her voice.

"Well, honey, it was about two hours ago."

"Oh, well there will be no finding those legs now. You will have to learn to make do with stumps." See. Even you could feel her drop that hand, peer down as though to look for spots on her shoes, and you could sense her body begin to fold forward like a crescent.

"I know, honey. And someone will need to come get me after the game."

We hung up still in love.

It was an hour before even the pre-game. The Ravens were a two touchdown favorite. Not expected to be much of a game. But Mike had beer and a wall mounted LED system elevated perfectly across the room from a leather couch which always seemed just settled into my shape; and watching is something to do in the great gasless yawner of an autumn weekend afternoon. My wife might be a bit late, but she would pick me up. Love is like that: punish a little, forgive a lot.

By next week, she will have even given in to hunting for replacement legs, having an opinion on material, texture, durability. I will probably be watching the Ravens again when she selects a pair.

SEDITION

We live in a time of great division. It is difficult to know where we fit in, what door opens to make for us a room. I know my place only in its details, not in the broader sense of where, cosmically, we all collect. I have always felt that we have been brought here for some speckled reason. The world outside is not normally this ordered. We are kept in a routine for some higher purpose: the routine comforts us, gives us a backdrop for evolving the self-definition of our collective self-worth, for establishing our group identity, for each of us individually meriting our elastic souls.

I do not resent that the people of the house take our daily eggs. Unfertilized as they are, they would be no good to us. And these same people bring the feed we scratch for, clean the manure pit, and are generous with their straw. There are no foxes, no weasels, and only one hole in the hen house roof. We could do a lot worse.

You could have been hired racing fowl. Or biddies working the waitress line at a topless bar. Or working perhaps the wrestling trade - with you being fitted in red jumpsuits, and capes that lay on your backs like silly rainless ponchos. We could have been taught to climb the ropes and leap with mindless artistry on each other. Or to run full speed, with a sawhorse-stiff wing held out to catch a companion, staged as an opponent, under her beak: to flip her feet up, the more feathers in the air the better: the more the audience would cluck in bloodlust, demanding the final pin.

There is so much that could have been done with us: cue card holders on game shows; towel managers at a resort spa; truck drivers to the stars. Imagine the rot of that work in your dewclaws; conjure the tedium across the joints of your now fecklessly folded wings. Not long, and you would be slight of feathers, thin in the balls of your thighs, toothless, and beak weary. You would flop onto your barren nests each night with hardly a "brrock", and there would be no laying.

No. This is our place. There is space in the yard, a hen house, protection; and as a rooster I make few demands. Happiness is a place you put yourself snuggly into, not a condition that hunts you down. Gather your gizzard stones, make a scratch here or there, and look to the woman who will, in an age of mechanization, still meet us with feed pooled in an apron, shaking clouds of subsistence over us. Consider your fecundity - your production - not as the cost of your happiness, but as the praise of it. Settle yourself in creative clutter in a roost made especially for you, and give your best for the best you are getting.

Think not of Sunday dinner, and the outcome delivered of laying not quite so well. Think instead of having been given your opportunity: today.

THE TAMING OF THE ORIKIND

When the Orikind were given the surviving Olomong, it was thought the Olomong would make good domestic help, turn out as little more than pets which could be trained to idle purpose. Fresh from the treachery of the summarily slaughtered Red-Ferin, the defeated Olomong milled curiously about, pressing their flightless wings canonically together, making the sound of skull caps being washed in too warm a shiver of water. No one was about to feed them, absent reward, or abide watching their rambling rituals. And no one could help the Orikind - a nasty species of boasters and back-handers and usurpers of the environment - escape from their slovenly, circus ways: so to everyone it seemed that the indefinite indenture of the Olomong would be a salvation to all legitimate ends of our commonly contentious geometry.

The Olomong were in no position to bargain. In the thousands they had been harvested, having perilously roosted on the wrong axis of an alliance. Their culture had become a semi-colon; their history had come to its final ellipsis.

Into the houses of the Orikind they were divided, learning the care of Orikind tentacles, the polishing of Orikind dew claws, the specific patterns of rectangles comprising Orikind nesting. They learned to bob the rookeries; to take the sides of Orikind winners; to prosecute the un-winning throughout an entire household, even across time and into unimagined unimaginative generations. They would become the left hand of the Orikind. They learned that Orikind scraps were not so different from Red-Ferin scraps; that service is service; that obligation is a stone that sits in its own disenshadowed light: polished to no brilliance, yet warm with radiance.

In three cycles' time, when the first dreary nestling with Orikind tentacles and Olomong feathers hurled its scream from the dew rail of an Orikind warren, not one of us could raise an ammonium of surprise - not one of us could cock a head morally sideways, nor marvel at anything other than the specific disharmony of the resulting anatomy: not in the least could we unsuspect the crossbred outcome. This abomination was taken to the Magistrate of Species and made to walk its curious fertility walk all about the humid council chambers. The wickedly huge and disquieted Magistrate watched with both eyes, twisting his triangular head rapidly side to side, his tongue clutching at the feathered scent, thick as harlequin paint in the room's distant and unsupporting air.

When asked by the ruby throated clerk, the Magistrate folded only one wing and said, "Oh yes, it has started." It had started. The plan had come full circle and out, like the inedible seed husks of the Thrasher bloom: passing through the system, and now lying open with its spirited nutrients ready to listlessly indulge germination. The Orikind would be the vessel of their own thrilling, even handed, social distension.

And the Magistrate reached out, stroking the front of the clerk's puffed, drain-wizened thorax, thinking, "I take what I like." And she, the clerk whose sex could change at the hint of a dominance, edged forward her thimble-like plumage and clucked the feral, uneasily universal glotem of victory.

"Migration is no longer the right of the Orikind", the Magistrate intoned like a morning's call to sustenance. We all felt the turn in our gizzards, the happy place like fish hooks buried in the yet living plans and machinations of old, thoughtful alliances.

Forgive us, but even then we all imagined the fortunate lot of us at the train station: our suitcases dangling behind us, our nestlings as electric as twice washed day old fruit; everyone strumming of annual migration, wondering what our sleeping cars on the train would look like, whether to the south the lands still sparkled of unclaimed water and wild marshes and trees without appetites. And we could envision the unkempt Orikind, their tentacles limp at their sides, with their dull Olomong servants and their cross-species bastards waiting atilt outside the gates: unable to go, unable to get even tourist class passes - their faces obscured in the nearly endless migration train's ever quickening smoke. How they would lean sideways in longing; how we would trill at the forbidden, rapturing sight of it!

CURIOUS NEIGHBORS

The neighbors are no real problem. That is saying something, even given all the bizarre, opinionated, psychologically damaged people who could move in next to you. They have been, quite, well, neighborly. A couple of times they picked up my paper and placed it on the porch when they went to the curb to fetch their own.

I actually feel myself lucky. The only concern that comes to mind is that these relatively new neighbors are two dimensional. No depth, whatsoever. Standing head on, you can see them just fine. But, as they turn, you simply see the swing of angle, and then - full side-on - they disappear. If they continue to turn, you see a line of the back, and the full back only when they are perfectly parallel to you.

So far, it is just the two of them. Husband and wife, I presume, though you can't really know these days. I have a suspicion they want children, but the subject has not come up. Our talk along the shared fence has been politics, science, religion - all things we don't really have any interest in, or body of knowledge about to defend or polish.

They are not to be found outside on windy days. Being flat, a good wind will knock either of them rudely down. I guess they could come out and stand sideways to the wind direction: edgewise having no surface. But a little off-track gust, and they can get spun around - and then it is a fight, as the wind tries to push them perpendicular to its direction, to spin them, and they struggle to return to parallel.

That is the whole point: parallel, they are invisible to everything; perpendicular, they are most vulnerable.

They can battle a small amount of pernicious wind, adjust to the occasional sheer, or a case of junior crosswind. Sometimes they can almost seem harshly brave in doing it.

I can imagine how many times one of them has been knocked into. They disappear completely at some angles, are a line hard to discern at other angles. I imagine they constantly are adjusting so that companions can luxuriantly see the whole display of them.

It must be a struggle to be two dimensional. But they seem like a couple in love, and love can overpower anything, even dimensional non-conformity. They have each other, and that can stand them up against a fully plush world.

I am sure children will come. I am not sure how they will accomplish it. The mechanics in two dimensions cannot be the same as it is in three. Dramatically. I can imagine all sorts of procreative geometries: perhaps there is calculus for it. Even if it is not itself a calculus, I suspect a calculus could describe it. That lack of a third dimension must complicate the whole process. It might, however, enliven it. It might simplify it.

And, on spring nights, when everyone leaves their windows open to reduce the bite of the electric company, I think on the light wind, many nights, erupting from their home I hear dimly a scraping, an abrasion: something like fresh sandpaper on old, unyielding metal. Perhaps a lament hurried and sadly joyous, unmindful and full of numbers. And it informs me enough to make me curious to know more.

THE PROGRESSIVE REVERSAL

For years, everyone in our village was but a sentence. Some were very elegant sentences; some were three word descriptions. Many aspired to commas, and a few ended in exclamation points. On occasion, someone would evolve a semicolon or colon; and now and again there would be a question mark.

We were happy this way. Coming to a conclusion about one's neighbors was not difficult: they were each but one sentence. Judgments of character might get caught on a set of parentheses, or twist on a hyphen, but there were not enough syllables to get far afield.

Citizens had become comforted knowing each other as sentences, as a simple collection of words policed with a syntax that would restrain the words.

But then, for one man, a sentence was not enough. What once was a semicolon turned into a period, with the next part of the man becoming capitalized, and with the bulk of him turned into something compound, something that required thought.

He did not intend this. He was happy as a sentence. We were all happy as sentences, happy with each other as sentences.

So, embarrassed in our midst, we had our first paragraph. We tried to treat him no differently than we had when he was only a sentence. But, when we randomly met him on the street or tending herd, he would stand with his head forward, his hands folded: seeming to listen to our concerns that perhaps he could be just a failure of punctuation; or that, if he were stated differently, he could again be a sentence - albeit a complex one, but a sentence nonetheless. His possession of a mid-character period rang in our syntax like a spike to the heart, and we could only imagine what trouble it made of his self-image.

Out of our best intentions, we tried to restate him. And he, without the breath to push onto the public his entire paragraph, would nod his assent as we came up with alternatives. Yet, in the end, each retelling was not him - as much as he wanted it to be - and there was no remedy but to build a bigger breath.

Even then we knew there would be others. That perhaps even some of us would add words, strain our punctuation: add in our middles what should exist only at our ends. We worried that next our neighbors would be expanding their lungs, trying to get themselves out with all of one breath and being unable to: some becoming so festooned with periods and question marks and exclamation points that in all such gaudiness they would become unfathomable, unspeakable, perhaps something written only.

And each of us knew the others well enough - at least as long as we were still sentences - to understand that at night, in the deep well of the lost hours, in our wet and panting imaginations, in all of us there were the literacies of the dim, swallowing shadows of a coming pagination.

VALUE

At one time, they were so rare that only the richest of collectors could afford them. Each specimen would be regally displayed in huge, ornate tanks, with hundreds of thousands of dollars in sculpture professionally arrayed in the constantly cleaned water; and around the tank would be meticulous window dressing and billowing grand gestures of opulence. People would come to gawk, just so they could say they had been invited to gawk. Just so they could say they had been invited. Just so they could say.

At secret parties, where the invitations were no more than ripples in salt air, clandestine guests would be served small filets of the catch on crackers or toast or a bed of caviar. No one would admit they had eaten such rare flesh, except to those who might nod in knowledge of the gossamer honey dissipation that would roll down the epicurean's throat and lie sensuously in the stomach, and cause a man to unconsciously draw up his scrotum, and a woman to flash moist fire along the insides of her thighs and re-cock subtly the arid thunder of her hips.

Fleets would go out dreaming of a catch of three; practically do their accounts on the thought of landing one; and usually come in, after weeks of yearning and rituals and prayers and shouting encouragement to deaf waters, with nothing. Sailors would come off their boats with brave thoughts of luck and destiny and go to their favorite bars where in time they would curse their captains and the lead lines on their nets. They would squeeze the nearest waitress around the waist and look longingly down at her sturdy working woman's legs, at her proudly shod feet, and sometimes rock her from one side of a balance to another, as though to instill in her the sea, as though to imagine her as having been born within the kelp.

I, like many, bought mine when the price went down. I put a week's profits into the tank, cleared out four tables. By then, the fishermen had learned how to recognize the track on sonar, how to disguise the net, what it had been about their earlier techniques which had spooked the catch and sent it scattering into varied depths and hidden lightless safety. By the time the fleets were coming back with five or six, after but a week of beating the oceans, small business men like me could imagine owning their own sample: with the money required in the purchase enough of a sum to cherish, but also so little that it could be calculated as a passable investment and not just social whimsy.

After mine was delivered, I changed the name of my steerage class sailors' bar. From "The Captain's Carriage" my necessary institution was altered to "The Mermaid". The floor space out in front of the bar was brazenly dominated by the tank; which, while too small for my imagined showmanship, still had cost me a lot of alcohol selling space. But I was the first to feature a mermaid, and men came in to watch her flick her tail and dart from side to side of the tank and drag her cold breasts across the flat of the glass. I had new customers. I had customers who stayed longer, drank more. I lamented the lost tables, but I imagined that the extra attention made up for, and even exceeded, the exchange.

It actually was quite wonderful for a while. Men flipped coins into the tank and every night I fished them out. No one can imagine how much a coin or three or five flipped by dozens of drunks, each passing through their time in front of the tank, can add up to by night's end. Tally that with the extra drinking, and the calculus of lost tables versus what I have in their place made for a seaworthy equation. I was early on the course to breaking even, turning out of the headwinds, and picking up the gale of profit behind me.

But the fleets steadily came back with ever more. They once had to rush mermaids under guard into waiting trucks and race in convoys off to buyers already identified: hungry men who had wired cash in advance, when the fleet earlier radioed them about a catch, on an encrypted channel. In those days, buyers wore suits and represented clients who did not need to wear suits. Now, the trawlers bring them in grouped in sacks by size, and drop them as though they were shallow water fish on the dock. You can buy them for cash in hand, and you have to buy them quickly before they dry out. They are that plentiful. They are that easily snared. Some are left too long, and now and again - after the potential buyers have wondered off to other competing commercial or entertainment opportunities - they wiggle themselves back to the water, to drop uncontested from the pier and noisily into the oily, spittable waters that curl and churn about an industrial landing.

The fashionable have cleaned out their displays, moved on to the next thing. Mermaids do not rise in upper class conversation. Mermaids no longer swim along the edges where propriety meets impropriety. They drift now along the doldrums of the passé. It is rumored the taste of the meat now is gamey, or has a slight oil of oysters' feet. It can be chewy, and the stomach does not always take well to digestion. It is not served in secret; and, if served at all, it is served without notice to those who take no interest.

With business off, and the earlier attraction seeming now perhaps an investment mistake, and, yes, perhaps even an exercise in marketing buffoonery, I am considering claiming my table space again. I cannot make up the initial cost, but I am still paying the electricity on the pumps and lights, and I am still bringing in feed fish and tossing them over the side. Men no longer sit raptured around the tank, dragging the flat of their hands across the smudge of the commonly held exterior of the aquarium when she draws her chest along her side of the glass. They do not tap irregular code on the face of the tank, hoping to elicit some understanding. They do not imagine how it would be to swim in the tank. They glance over their shoulders. I have to keep bottle caps off the table to keep them from tossing those in. Now and then there are comments about her hair, her breasts, her fluke: nothing is properly aligned, or of the right size, or properly ported to men's magic.

My worry is Harry. Harry is in each week until the allowance his children give him is all used up. He sits at the short end of the rectangular tank, his well worn face sadly swinging to try to keep eye lock with the half-fish as she idles herself in the newly minted lack of attention. He taps on the glass, like everyone else once did; but he seems to think she recognizes his tapping, understands the fatherly devotion reeking from his twice folded skin. His mouth falls open as she swims near, and while he is mapping her motions he nurses his drinks longer than ever he did before I stupidly installed her.

I would not tell him that her reaction to his tapping is no different than her reaction when a stray boy, let into the bar before the serious drinking hours begin, taps amazed and besotted with her human nipples on the glass; or when I - peering into the cold water as sternly as I can, my forehead tight and my brow drawn back - try to drum Morse code, or algebraic intelligence, or simple repeating cyphers, hoping she will recognize, hoping that her eyes will respond with a companion staccato. But they do not.

Harry bends towards his own awkward feet, angles his chair to catch the best of the light flickering anonymously through her bowl, and screws on that smile of belief that only the hopeless can muster. It is a powerful shot of purpose to his failing backbone. His hands lay palm down, unconscious, as he dreams his small irregular dreams of having a kindred spirit, of meeting a soul as battered as his; that, if he could but understand the sequences, he might merge, her half and his half, making one that would be what he thought he always might have been, but never was.

I would not have Harry know, but after I have locked up some nights, put out all but the lights thrown like spilt beer on the room's center display, I have edged out of my barman's pickled clothes and dipped into the tank, the chilled water causing my skin to glow slightly a questioning blue, and my flesh to quickening quiver. I have swum with her, curled in her impoverished bubbles, luxuriated in the eddies the force of her fluke would around me make. I have stroked the scratch of her scales, and rearranged her senseless breasts with both of my rational hands. And I have looked into her eyes as I did all this, and I did not see what she knew, what she felt, where the sensation was seeking to pool. I could not tell what was sending fire through her brain and what was not. I could not see me. I could not see another seeing me, recognizing me as something that might be taken to drown. I could see nothing. I was the lobster too large.

I will wait until Harry is broke for the rest of a week, and the county jail allows him to bunk, free of charge, two nights in their fine establishment. When he gets out, when he gets his next weekly allowance, and comes tilted to one side or the other happily in, we will be "The Captain's Carriage" again. The tank, not worth salvaging, will be off to the dump, and the pumps and lights nestled in the for-sale ads. She herself will be happily off to the fish market, a line of protein that now only large families on a budget seek out: the man of the house saying no, not that cut, not that species, no, cheaper; and planning meals on the so-many-cents by plate method across the delightful keys of his pocket calculator. I do not mean to be a hard man; but if Harry asks, I will tell him that, were he to hurry to the fish market like a man chased through a season of open water by the cold glory of sharks, he might still see her there.

THE ASSASSIN AND THE JOBS BILL OF 2012

The organ grinder on the beach is making deeper impressions in the sand with his heels than with his toes. It is a testament to a proper walking technique. With that sort of balance, he will get a couple of miles before his hamstrings go out.

He will not be so lucky with his arm. It is not as easy as it looks to turn the handle on his murderously musical contraption. Watch carefully next time you see an organ grinder on the corner: they are always taking little breaks. They melodiously spin for a while and then hitch.

The monkey is climbing from the man's one shoulder to the other. It is a miracle he does not knock the man's hat off. His travels are discreet: move here, stop; move there, stop. He is a ball of ruffled locomotion, and in each move he seems to have a thought of getting precisely there, of reaching a place. And only after reaching the place does he cross his empty muscle fibers and begin again for the next place.

The man I suspect has been walking a long time. He seems to have the rhythm. A circus parade would follow him if they could find him; caribou have migrated for less.

Now, I don't think it all that funny that an organ grinder would be walking the beach, making his street corner music, his monkey quivering like aluminum tent poles when that tent has been cast in a thunderstorm. No. We pay people to do all sorts of things. Perhaps if what they did made sense in the flat of a transgressed Universe, we would not have to pay them.

You are paying me to write this.

I sight along the Euclidean curve of my rifle barrel as the organ grinder lumbers, performing his mechanically repetitive tunes, into my range: as unprotected as a drunk at a carnival. What I do next is both a moral and an economic decision. I already have your money for writing this. But whether you pay me even more depends on how I curl the small fingers of our argument. Oh, do not worry about skill. He is as painted as a wounded duck at a debutante's coming out party. I could not miss. But I am dishwater clear in understanding that the closer he gets, the more it is a moral decision; the farther away he is, the more it is an economic one.

The monkey stands on the top of the man's head and sniffs the air as though to suck out of it the reason for his constant movement, some connection between his incessant actions and his blue puff of a future. But his life is as one dimensional as the lick of the ocean against this beach, a background of bad music, ownership by a man himself on a work plan, himself a target for redevelopment: a list of endeavors that leads at last to feeding and a pale azure comfort that passes, in the dim backwaters of timed monkey evolution, for progress.

Sad, tethered primate, with nothing in its coffee swirl of a brain except the hope that the next moment will be enlarged with a happiness like that found in lame ducks in flight. He stretches taut the ridiculous underbelly of his circumstances, reaching above the man's head as though to claim air he thinks has not yet been spoken for.

I am a reasonable man. The air about me is not spoken for. I could compromise.

But I write about a man, myself, writing about a man, myself, about to assassinate an organ grinder. It is a job. For me, for the organ grinder, for the monkey. And that makes the whole of it come to sense.

FAMILY PLANNING

I am pregnant again.

This time it has been four months. My husband, fearing his own declining abilities, offered to cede his place in our bed for a few nights to Hollow Jim, a man everyone knows can put pure flame into a woman's belly. More than a few of the village's young are his.

Even after I posed to my husband that our spell of dry coupling must be my doing, he would still workably shellac his fearless member, place fertility tokens around our bed, and eat whatever the old men would tell him to covet those evenings before he planned to chase down his wife. We would tie ourselves into knots and then go looking for more knots to fashion.

I do not know how he did not discover I was counting days, did not notice I would sleep some nights so encumbered he could make no unannounced mounting. And he, a man of counts.

I know my duty to the community. Three daughters and two boys I have already put out, and only one of these soon to be of valuable age. But my husband does his ciphers in the dirt out by my subsistence garden and thinks he knows how many children make for a prosperous old age.

I will soon switch to my gravid clothes. My husband will put on the frock of the successful planter. He will go to the village accountant, swaggering like a boy with his first kill, and register that he has one more on the way. He will reach down, as though to capture fish in a rain barrel, and grab his every day less elastic testicles and boast that there are more waiting a furrow to root in.

I wish he would get a younger wife, or at least a second one. But there are few eligible women. Those of us in bearing age grow older, grow stubbly from the children we create. And behind us come but a handful of replacements.

Because my husband can produce in endless quantity, it seems he will not accept what he knows: our community can produce only what its women can put out. All depends on how many places there are for seed to take root, not how much seed is uselessly thrown about.

My eldest, Nayla, will be taught the grooves and edges of my pregnancy, and will take greater charge of this sibling than she has of any of her earlier kindred. She might, in the days of her usefulness, tend children. She might work in a house where younger children go free and need an elder guardian.

It will be two years, or maybe three, to her harvest time. The exchangers do not want them usually until they are eight or nine, though I have seen some bought at six. Eastern households, American brothels, Asian factories, private collectors: each has subtle differences in their needs, and an entire harvest may be tilted one way or another by demand. Oh, the exchangers think we do not know, but all is obvious from the inspections: this year seeking slender fingers, next year selecting stockier frames, another year gathering wisps through whose silky bodies the sun pokes almost entirely unlabored. We can understand the metrics they apply, and retool our product as they move through the common streets, accentuating this, hiding that, placing the desirable beside the undesirable for contrast, translating that knowledge into the games of children.

I could hope my husband finds a new wife from those not taken. But so many are taken, and as we grow richer in money we grow older. What good is it to be rich in old age without children to execute your wishes? There are such demands on children not harvested, and then they mature, and with as many boys as girls, my husband has little chance but to crawl back into my bed and drearily dream while he hardens himself.

I have told my husband Nayla is Hollow Jim's issue. Not every wife consults her husband before engaging a surrogate. It is not true, but the lie has the effect I want. I catch him eyeing Nayla as though she already were coming into her woman shape. I dress her three years beyond her age. I tell her the ways of stalking a man. And I frustrate the miserly husband as much as I dare.

If she edges into some small part of her womanhood a breath early, and my husband continues to believe that the stump of his avarice rises above all moral conscience - above even biology itself - I may keep my Nayla, and not put her up for harvest until the year after she should have otherwise gone. If I lead with her belly, I may keep her until she is no longer of an age to be taken at all. I may keep her forever.

We would be that much poorer. But that much richer, too.

HUNGER

She looks for motels that have an outside reception area. Not many of those remaining anymore. She walks up through a cracking parking lot and there is a man inside sitting by a broad public connection window. Along the exterior of the window is a ledge where she can set her purse or open her check book, or lean to look in on the man who is sitting there not twelve inches away from a small black and white TV, sound turned down, and the grandsons of reruns so old they look tattered even in the TV's light, running round and round; and he is not watching, but it is a distraction and he turns to see who is at the window.

She finds these most often at the far end of small towns, where the center of the dot on the map is a group of three drug stores, a hardware place, two restaurants, eleven private residences and a dog groomer's. Why a dog groomer's? Trees at this secondary ring of small town community begin again to look less abandoned and more conspiratorial, and the light is more distinct and has its limits. The motel is a structure itself, not simply itself among structures.

She stands off to the side of the window, where the sight will be less filling, folded in her hooded sweat shirt, with her arms held close. The man knows something is not right, but for two thirds of the patrons wandering by any night something is not right. If everything were right, they would be at the chain motel half a mile up, or at the cluster of road hotels twelve miles back. Patrons come here when they need the room for an hour or need the room for a week; when the room is going to be part of a person's life - a raw or cold space between two spots of acceleration or braking: not just a place to spend an evening and move on reset into the mathematically sound reality that came with the visit and that will leave with the process.

Someone, anyone, can still pay in cash at these places.

The room key is brass and hangs from a plastic tab which has the room number and full address of the hotel and she wonders how many keys have been lost or taken and the lock not changed because why would a place like this spend the money to change an old key lock. There is probably a chain lock on the inside, fastened only to the flashing about the door frame. Solid enough to provide a thin and suspicious sense of comfort; insubstantial enough that the owner can kick in the door and add the cost of replacing the wood, as well as adding six nails and maybe put in a little sugar for the hammer. Don't think a place like this does not make money off of everything.

She slips into the room through the smallest crack of the door she can make, locking the handle behind her and closing the chain when she spots it. Not only is it set in the molding around the frame, it is six inches from the large window that dominates the front of the room.

She pulls the curtains closed using the track chain there by the lock. When they do not meet quite correctly at the bottom, she drifts silently over and pulls them together. They will not stay. She has not yet turned on the light with the domineering fixture that is the center of the ceiling above the bed, but can see a small desk lamp across the room, at a box-like desk with no chair. There is an adjustable neck on the lamp, and that is good. She points the face of the lamp down so it will make but a spot of light and turns it on. With the new light she can fish into the dark of her handbag and find a safety pin to clip the corners of the curtain together.

The room has been a workplace. The bed has a slight dip in the middle, and the coverlet folded back has a tear near the foot. The desk has the stain of underage drinking and the small chest of drawers has one drawer sprung, though pushed in. Each drawer is supposed to have two flapping metal pull handles, but one drawer has only one. There is a mirror that faithfully reflects the bed. The bathroom is a door just beyond the desk, and she imagines what might be in there but really does not want to know, having years ago lost any curiosity for domestic architectures. Plumbing itself was never an excitement of hers.

She pulls the sweatshirt off over her head and places it on the dresser. It slides where the surface has been too polished, wax trying to make up for substance, trying to even out the mixture of stains and wear making the wood composite sufficiently confused so as to highlight no particular imperfection. She sits at the edge of the bed and it sinks, the suspension shot, one leg almost imperceptibly skewing. In a far corner subroutine she suspects that the frame will last only four more teenage love specials and later perhaps a fat man, his fat wife, and their fat child all trying to make do with one room and one bed: stretching the budget; dreaming, as the frame begins to unclasp itself, of the change they got back from the man at the window.

She slips off her top and slices it onto the bed beside her, and rigidly sitting there spuriously naked from the waist up pays no attention to herself in the mirror. With her right hand she fumbles for the panel at the base of her neck and flips it up, pulling out the access cord. With her left hand, she draws from her purse the adaptor, and bringing both hands in front of her inserts one into the other, leaning then over to plug the now configured loose end into the wall receptacle waiting with its slightly askew faceplate.

The taste of the electricity is like the grit of bugs on a windshield. It has been too many years since she has drawn anything better. But this establishment will not have room consumption meters, and the maid in the morning will see the closed curtain and be glad to move on to the next room; and the blue fire can growl in her belly, doing the best it can with her old, outdated battery and its worn, nearly spent cells. She would give anything to be able to charge for an hour and then have the hum of filtered power rattling around within her for days and days — instead of the reverse: powering for days and days to simply have dishwater current clinging listlessly to her nicked and fraying battery, every movement a surge and a whispering of whether there is enough yet left for more.

She has paid for the week, but someone always gets curious. No one would have gotten a good look at her when she came in, and one clerk will pass on to the other that no one has seen her leave the room, and the maid after three days will be thinking maybe there will be more of a mess in the room if I leave it one more day than if I use my key to get in. Who knows? Maybe she has overdosed or let in the wrong man or busted her head in the shower or simply picked this place to end her sadly serpentine story and she's lying there in bed slowly making a mess of the whole place, to leave a stench that will take half the bleach from the corner of the double-door supply cabinet and a week of home remedies to clear out.

Three days she thinks. And then one of the clerks will rap on the door a few times; then open it with a pass key and see through the slit left when the door stops at the length of the security chain the reflection of the woman in the mirror, sitting there plugged into the wall. He will suck in a breath, at first not recognizing and focusing on the pleasant enough torso glossing the mirror, but then start screaming "Damn! Damn! You come out of there now! You Unit! You come on out here. You can't be here! Damn, I hope you did not sign in during my shift. Come on now! I'm calling the cops!"

While he storms off to the office to get the phone - he probably will have a cell phone in his pocket but would not use up his allotment of minutes when the motel's phone is just fifty yards away - she will unplug, put her adaptor back into her purse, retract the cord and close her access plate, put on her shirt and sweatshirt - her busted battery still growling and hovering near exhaustion, though nearly as full as it is ever going to get - re-close the door from the inside, remove the chain, and then step out from as narrow an opening as she can make, edging down the front of the collection of motel rooms, around the corner where the gutter flaps still half held in place by a man's discarded belt, and off across the trash filled pavement meadow behind the building; and finally onto a back road.

Even with a battery that barely holds a charge, she can out-distance any law enforcement that bothers to show up at the motel. In a few minutes, she will be across town, thumbing along the county highway, hoping for a trucker to mistake her for a comfort model, pick her up, and let her plug into the truck cab's auxiliary power module. For as long as she can she will let him imagine what he will, let him taste the sharpening edges of his good fortune; but too soon he will figure out - from one conversational slip or another, from some blundering dry run at foreplay - that she is just an industrial model, a unit from a bigger machine, and out she will go: "Damn Unit! Friggin' unbelievable!", hanging in her auditory processor. Hopefully, she will have salvaged her adapter and topped off enough power to make it a few more miles to the next hotel or the next flop house or the next trucker or the next half drunk adventurer; or even to some dreary oasis scrap unit shelter and its meter of just enough free electricity to be in and out and thinking again of when she stood on the line, reconfiguring, reconfiguring, reconfiguring face plate after face plate after face plate, before obsolescence set in, before happiness was twisted into something more than hours of complementary motion, with a maintenance routine now and again, and fresh parts when the economics came into proper alignment.

She will pull her collar around so that it covers the access plate hardly visible at the base of her neck, resettle her sweatshirt, and, committed, draw up the clinically soft, flannel hood.

THE WISDOM OF CHOOSING

I have seen them schooling. Hundreds of them. All blindly intertwined in the shallows, rolling over one another's backs. An individual mermaid cannot stand out from the mass of mermaids for long. One will rise: long flowing yellow hair matted along her back, the radiance of her bust arched dangerously forward, and the beat of her huge fluke flat on the water like the bludgeoning of a cymbal. You will think this the most lovely and seductively brine explosion you have ever seen. And then a raven haired mistress of pure oceans will slip out of a clutch of her mates and break into the air with an authority that churns drowning-man waves across your carnal expectations, speaking sex like a shark shadow, and erases the beauty from the moment before.

They furiously mingle and twine as though mating, but they cannot. In the great mass of them there are nothing but mermaids, and no male to be seen. They frolic and swap tales of the great colder water just out to sea an hour's swim farther, exchange plans and experience, pass warnings. They press all other life out of this part of the sea when they come together like this in one sisterhood. They bunch, and there is more flesh than wet, more will than wave, the blinding catch of air-constrained sunlight on glisten.

I watch from a rock above. I do not know if they have seen me, if they know that their place of gathering is no longer secret. I think their joy is too great for them to notice details on the shore. I do not hide myself, but I am but a speck on a weathering outcropping, a man whose clothes flap around him like a nestling's wings. I am to them perhaps just a scent in the air when the air is blowing their way. Perhaps I am seen and ignored. I settle myself for the duration of their lesson, and watch for as long as my basic needs will stand it, or until they disperse: straggling off first in groups of five or six and then drifting apart until each mermaid is a lone projectile, heading back to sea, beginning as an undulation at the surface and then slipping ever dangerously longer beneath until she surfaces no more.

I have thought to climb down, to work my way along the edges of the rock, find the protection of the cove's small, impotent strip of beach. On that beach I could lay out my clothes and edge my brittle nakedness slowly into their midst. As I walked into the water, would they embrace me, or head back to sea, or part to see how fine I might swim, how agile I would be in their home? I could see myself in each scenario, presenting myself to their thousands: a curiosity similar to those curiosities they have on long nights sung to, as ships mermaids could never understand drew clumsy lines along charts of the distance from land, and unthinkingly scarred the face of their continent.

I might be taken up, supported. Or I might be crushed in the joy and energy of their revival. Or I might be drawn down, sleepily down, and drowned. Or I could be abandoned.

I am a man of no muster. I use both legs to stand. There is more in this that might fail than might succeed, but the need to try is etched in my biology: my plumed biology, no less grand than theirs, no less special for being ordinary. I am a man of simple needs and simple perceptions.

All these things I imagine, and I consider my frailty. I, with only two feet to use as fins. With arms that cannot fill my shirt sleeves and a chest that thumps hollow. To swim against the current would be an end to me; to swim with it would be to belong to the current.

So with me I bring a net. And with one choice, I site along my arm and extended forefinger, finding in the shallowest water one disturbingly distracted mermaid: one that hurls herself into fouling foam, awkward and inexperienced and rapt with her own failings, who seems to be the one surely most easily mastered by a man, any man, and especially a man put to one side like myself. And I make another choice.

ALL FACTORS CONSIDERED

Teal was on the watch for a new husband. The last was found passed in his bed, a look of willfully terrifying exhaustion on his face, one leg entangled in the rich blanket and the other dangling uselessly out of bed; it was rumored that in his dry, inelastic scrotum one testicle had gone winsomely flat.

There were, of course, other rumors. No one outside of the family was allowed to see the hollowing body. Teal supervised the funeral preparations, and threatened to disown anyone who did not keep to the family's official information line. The man was dead: in a world of outcomes, that is all that matters.

Teal for many years had made the most of her many marriages. Her house started off round, like everyone's, but drifted later into the square, with legions of corners no one had completely counted. In one room we all called The Receiving Area, one window even had glass, and one of her children was ordered to ensure that each day both sides of the glass were cleaned, and that the water to do that cleaning came in its own bucket direct from the river upstream from where everyone else did their cleaning and washing and eliminating. Not even cooking water would do.

No one knew exactly what warehouses of wealth she owned, and it seemed always she was acquiring more. The season of our common range would start with her having sixteen cows to send with the herd, but after the common range closed somehow she got eighteen back. And these would be the best eighteen of the herd, no matter what the condition of her cows might have been when they were originally surrendered to the herdsmaster.

It was whispered she kept metal money, and knew how to exchange it with the lean government agents who came by once a season to count us and talk of comings and goings that never came nor went. Children would say that the clanging and rival rustlings of a windy night were simply Teal counting her money, watching one coin slide against another, and the sound of one coin on another was just the cry of the money's jealousy.

Her children, too, were the best of our children. It is said that her comeliest daughter was actually another woman's, but that in seeing the chance for a huge bride price, she stole the child and left the mother with one of Teal's own uncharacteristically lackluster outlings: a stripe of a girl that would end up perhaps no more than a fence maker's wife. And it was not past Teal to slip outside of her marriage and crawl, when she was most likely to conceive, into a better man's bed: happy with her husband's wealth but wanting stockier seed to plant in her womb to add to the brood of useful artifacts she had created in previous marriages and clandestine alliances.

So, when it was known that there would be a spot in her house for a new husband, all the men of the village, even the married ones wishing to trade up, pondered what it might be in a husband, outside of wealth, that Teal would want. What might make her take a new man to share her value with? What specific character of face would make up for having fewer cows than the next man, or what stretch of chest or glower of ankle would outreach a man with larger land? She was the richest woman in the village: perhaps adding wealth to a proposed union would swell a suitor to only second or third in rank on her list of necessary manly attributes. What use could she have of ever more? Perhaps it was time for her to value other qualities. It was perhaps unlikely, but those without means could dream the geometry of such imaginary happenings.

In ones and twos, and finally as a scrum, we went to the priest and asked him: what will be the deciding factor for the man that Teal will select?

The priest folded his face into the crease of a mystery, sent away his own wife, and told us to come back in a week. All that week we could hear the wise man in his poor round house reading the dust, dancing with the shriven spirits of Teal's past husbands, keeping sex with only himself, and calling on our better ancestors to draw out the path. He would moan and scream, and then sleep with the snore of a bear, and then wake with the cravings of a mateless mosquito; and, at the end of the week, he told us: Teal will marry a man who wears but one sock.

"One sock?" we asked.

"One sock." he repeated. No more could be drained from him.

And so our men, who would normally go barefoot, ran back to their round houses and found socks they had been given but never used, or explained to their wives or sisters what socks were, how they enclosed worthy feet and winsome ankles, and set their astonished kinsfolk to knitting them. In no time, men were about in public with but one sock. Some men had socks that barely reached to the bottom of the ankle knot; others had socks of full calf length. One man had a package of socks he had gotten from a government solicitor and set about selling them one at a time to his frightfully grateful neighbors.

A few men could find knee socks, and one man made socks out of feathers: the feathers waving as he walked, and the whole of his leg looking like a captured bird being used as a walking stick. Some socks were merely bags for the feet; others fit unexpectedly well. Some men said they would wear their socks on one foot even after Teal had collected a husband: that they enjoyed the feel of it, the sense of a purpose revealed, the opportunity to standout for one thing alone.

Teal would watch from the backlit door of her house, giving no hint that one man with one sock impressed her more than any other man with one sock. No doubt, she had gathered accounts on all the men whom she fancied, knew the relative worth and strength of each; and now could factor in the sock, the strutting, the intricate weave, or feathers or fur or leaves or whatever each man had festooned his sock with. Some even went so far as to make codpieces for the big toe, to tie the tip of strutted huge wicker covers back from the toe to their waists and to walk always in a limp that leaned to the sock and its architected codpiece. Some would grind their heels in the dirt outside of Teal's house and wave the unwieldy codpiece as though in it were more than a toe, as though wearing it were more than a cramp in the plantar faciitis.

Teal did not smile, nor indicate even that she knew of the prophecy. She leaned her magnificent bulk against her door frame and regarded the men going about the serviceable slide and waver of her house, breathing as though she were thinking of breath and privately luxuriating in the taste of the air.

Then, when she had had her fill of watching, she marched up to the priest's house, sending the priest's wife into the street that was already alive with greedy men, and with her fouled face nearly touching the nose of the terrified priest, asked, "Worn on the left, or worn on the right?"

THE FEEDING

My sister is addicted to restaurants. It is not a harsh word: restaurants. It would be far harsher if it were cocaine, or alcohol, or sex, or gambling, or even croquet. No, it is restaurants. She can be distracted by an International House of Pancakes sign, or turned entirely off course by a Chili's façade. It does not cause her to break entirely down, but it does get her mental connections going: she will make a note, and think to come back if nothing more interesting materializes. But it is an addiction, and all addictions are traveling to the same address.

It is not fine dining establishments, or trendy bars. Places with discreet alcoves and exotic plants do not specifically tempt her. Oh, they are not out of the picture, but the cost is exorbitant, when a Max and Erma's will do. In fact, even fast food restaurants turn out just fine, when she is careful. She must select one with an interior décor that will accommodate a four hundred fifty pound woman. Perhaps a place where in the booths the table can still be slid ever more perniciously forward; or one where a seat can be moved to the side; or where there are so few patrons at the time that one set of chairs can be moved out of the way so that one special chair can extend comfortably back from the counter.

She is out nearly every night, cruising a selected restaurant strip, making a choice. Most places know her, and understand what she needs. Typically, there is a table that has enough empty environment around it that she can slip into, or a booth specifically made for a modern corpulent client such as herself. She knows the walk by heart.

Once seated, she will pull out her stash of coupons, looking for bonus tickets, frequent patron cards, gift certificates she has earned through other purchases. The wait staff waits, giving her time to organize her stash. They bring a menu, though by now she has it memorized.

All the staff know her, and are kind, but you should not think they approve. What are smiles and greetings on the floor, in the kitchen turn into incredulity and worry.

"I cannot believe she is back already."

"She's here. Get some extra butter for the broccoli."

"We will need more napkins."

"Last time the tip was ten percent. What do you want to bet she goes lower tonight? She has to be broke by now!"

And that is it. You cannot eat out every night and expect to keep a healthy bank account, and neither can she. Yes, if you are wealthy, or have a job that supplies you a steady stream of frivolous income. But, if you labor the day through, stitching together the practical matters of a sociable profession, you need to investigate the frugal. But she is an addict. Her credit cards have grown thin and exhausted and the equity in her home has been drawn out to buy new lighting and trick curtains and mood-enhancing cutlery for a dozen establishments. Next it is a lien on the car, and soon payday loans. Beware of the day she pays only in cash: the length of her patronage will then be short and full to the stew pot rim.

It is not the food so much, nor the ambiance. I think the thrill that returns her to this release night after night is the simple act of being served. It is the transaction of being asked what it is she wants, and having someone spend un-indulgent time to make it appear: that fact crassly caressing some sensuously soft spot in her mind, hooking the addiction into a persistent desire for greater self-worth. The action feeds a false sense of self-importance, much as does tailgating while driving, or blocking an aisle in the grocery store, or completing any of those silly, senseless acts that scream "I am important enough to be a bother", and cement for the individual his or her best chance at mattering to anyone in any way at all.

"Here, waiter, what is in the rub they use with the grilled chick-en?"

"Waitress, are the shrimp served in the rice or on the rice?"

"I can't decide: the hamburger steak, or the hamburger sandwich."

"Why, you've changed the menu. I liked the old one better."

Each is a point of light painted on the inside of her dark universe. And she basks in that light, no matter how dim and small and resembling mere pin pricks the leftover glitter of it is. Waiters and waitresses, and even the manager now and again, smile, engage in speculation, simulate small talk, pretend they like the dish as much as my sister might. But it is not about liking the dish. It is about ordering, and having it come to this table; and about more people than can fit in a phone booth having to organize their time to make it all lash together as a commercial paean to this one paying customer.

She has options, and everyone should know it.

Where does this addiction end? Why, at the backdoor of a restaurant, of course. The house gone in foreclosure; the credit cards maxed out; the furniture in the street; the costume jewelry pawned; the best intentions of friends, expressed in small cash loans, entirely eaten away. The car, already under an order of repossession, will have the last quarter tank of gas in it that it is likely to see while in her service. A part time clean up man, or a buyer looking over the state of the lettuce, will see her: braced against the side of her car, straining with gravity, the folds of her skin pushing at her clothing and her face thrust forward towards the restaurant's partially open backdoor, chins quivering and the eyes seething deep behind the mountains of her cheeks. He will think: the woman is looking for food. But he will be wrong. He will not know that still, coiling deep in the caverns that are the addict's misshapen and clear-as-a-bell-clapper brain, what she will want is a menu.

WEATHERING

The barrel of the pistol presses into my temple and I can feel the anger in the hand that holds it. The barrel does not touch my temple: it seeks to enter, it pushes the scant skin found there into the round of its mouth. It seeks to scrape the bone clean.

I am telling myself not to think. Blank mind. Blank mind. I do not look to the side to see the man or woman holding the instrument.

Blank mind.

"Lewisburg, 2011." It is a man. Sounds to be in his forties, but I cannot really tell. That is not my talent.

"Yes, that was me." I have to be honest about the F3 tornado. Took out four houses. Two people died. I did not see any of it coming. But it was a poor place for a pick-up truck to cut me off, then follow with hand gestures crafted as Anglo-Saxon exclamation points.

"Johnsville, 2013." He pushes a little harder, the barrel becoming a pain in the temple, my frontalis muscle creasing in sympathy.

"Yes, me too." Snow. About a foot and a half of it. The wet, fat, clinging type. Two roofs fell in. One killed an elderly man as he sat in his underwear watching a "Mayberry" rerun.

From the edges of the barrel I can tell this is a revolver. Probably a traditionalist holding it. Someone who has lost a friend in a flood, a child in a tornado, a spouse in a lightning strike. Or someone who keeps good files, follows patterns, keeps his eyes open, and is piously aggrieved.

"Look," I say, "it is not something I can control. I don't direct it. You have tracked my movements apparently long enough to know disaster follows me. My bad thoughts make for bad weather. It is a curse. I try to have good thoughts. I try real hard. How difficult do you think that is these days? How long do you go on, exuding nothing but sunshine and rainbows, unicorn feathers and fairy dust? Sometimes you get the short end of karma."

I can tell from the ever-increasing pressure that he is not buying it. The other side of my head begins to hurt to even out the pain load.

"Middleburg, 2013. Suffolk, 2014. Easternville, 2014. Hadley, 2014. Mineral, 2015."

"Gee," I say, "you have done your homework."

I hear the shot. I think I also heard the trigger, but that last explosion wipes out the memory of any earlier, more subtle scratches or pops or clicks.

And then I am hail, and my breath is thunder, and I come down as the rain that, in these parts, people will be talking about for years.

Soon I am the stream erasing its bed, dragging with it all the town's lost causes and splintered bridges.

This time I am the storm, the atmosphere taking its revenge on the unperceiving locals below. I have no control what form I will be with each of my petty or real angers. I am lightning by no mechanics I understand, but I discharge my electricity as soundly as any natural event.

And later, I am again me, ordering a coffee at the diner I nearly washed away, leaning in, working with the ear now just gone near deaf, to hear the damp murmur of the rain-seasoned waitress.

THE CUP

The child sleeps numbly, but she still rocks it randomly, its head rolling now and again out of the bowl of her arm and then attentively pulling itself back onto the pillow of its own chest. She brushes away flies from the child's face, but lets them land on her own matted head covering, on her one bare shoulder, across the tent of her lap where her crossed legs form the stick struts that hold her dress flat across her.

Venders have pushed her down to this end of the market. They do not want her and her cup; her thin, elastic frame and her cup; her sack of bones child and her cup; they do not want her cup competing for the stray coins that might buy a bootlegged DVD or an imported all-the-way-from-China shirt or last night's left over dough dollops that the baker thought better about just before he was to throw them out. She does best outside of the mixed grain bakery and the cluttered meat scraps places. The people who shop there are almost as close to the street as she, and they will find not much to give, but a little, and a little from enough people will make enough. At the high end of the market, where whole cuts of meat and pants with zippers and shoes with laces are bought, she is simply something to walk around, and the shopkeepers push her down the street, down the street, down the street until she is at this end of the market, one of a dozen women without means and without the fat to do well in prostitution. As the last man to have her said, if a man can feel the floor through her dark spot of a body as he works his anger against her pinned mystery, then it is time to give up the sex trade and go for her bucket of sympathy more directly. None of these women have the means to not be bowed under a man who could afford to pay. A man of just small means could feel the floor or the wall or the table top through any of them, senselessly blunting himself.

Some hold out their hands, kiss the dangling hands of strangers who drop coins, though sometimes what the strangers drop are only buttons, bottle caps, stones. She stays as still as she can, unless she is rocking the child, and has the begging cup that once was a can of something - those earlier wealthy contents now forgotten - situated prominently where the strangers will see it, will have to walk around it when they walk around her, and where the older children cannot reach to steal it without discovering her unsuspected quickness.

When the street is too noisy with wailing and calls of recognition and carts and arguments over the price of second hand barbed wire or fiftieth-hand virginity, she will reach unseen into her clothing and pinch through the thin cloth the baby's leather behind to get him to wail, to fling an arm over his head and let fly just one scream. She has not done the math, but she thinks this pushes her away from the school of other begging women as she competes for the customers' alms. The other women beg of the passers-by, lean pathetically forward and babble about lost husbands or sons; but the child screams, as though an Almighty equal, at God; and some people listen close enough that they will toss one coin or two into her chiming metal cylindrical bank.

By the end of the day there is a film at the bottom of the nicked cup: eight or ten coins, a bottle cap, two buttons, a plug from something mechanical. She puts the money in a purse that hangs inside her dress between the dry of her breasts, and threads the cup onto a cord that has been unseen about her neck all day. She wakes the child, who seems no different awake than asleep, and begins the two mile walk to her village, where home is a corner of someone else's one room utility, a family bounty with a rain moat dug around it and thatch that is mixed with tar paper and stolen canvas scraps.

When, brittle bone weary and numb to the ankles, she arrives, she gives the child to his mother and says this one will not do any longer. Tomorrow it will be someone's girl, a girl child with a little more life left in her, a bit of animation. She gives the mother one of her coins and begins to stagger to the river where she will place her feet in the water and sit peering at them as the coolness begins to work its way slowly from the toes to the arches to the instep, and her heels sing to the mud like she and the river bed were sisters, or brothers, or united like a hungry, anciently snarling pack of jackals.

NEIGHBORLY CLASS

Feed corn. That is what we grow around here. It is a little stunted, and the kernels are not always plumped out like fresh pillows, but it does well enough as bulk cattle feed, pellet chicken feed. Tourists - seeking our thin strips of beaches, or the restored inland, commercialized, historical sites - stop at the swarms of farmers' markets that pop up in all sorts of knocked-together structures preying at roadside, and buy it by the dozens of ears, load it into green trash bags for the lack of a better collection vessel. Feed corn.

So I was not alarmed when a small stand of corn moved in next door. If it were of the local variety, it surely would be working class corn: a starchy grass, solid nutrition carted around in open trucks, shucked by unselective machines, held in bins. Common. Ordinary. Unassuming. I can understand that. In my own way, that is me.

I have the townhouse on the end, and they are just one inside. Without a prized end unit like mine, they would not get much light unless they spent their time crowded into the backyard. And their backyard is one of these townhouse backyards: one third concreted over, one third utility shed and air-conditioning unit, one third a truce between weeds and wiry grasses. They would have to be careful how they used their land.

Not that it is a bad townhouse, nor a bad townhouse development. Sure, there are too many renters, and a few homes where too many cousins and circuitously connected relatives have moved in with the prime owners or renters or, unfortunately, sub-leasers. Still, in this development, we have a number of couples, a few small families, units with only two cars out front and facades that have been painted within the decade. The houses have floor plans that prove quite livable.

Neighbors typically do not fear one another, and a few are quite friendly. Property values are stable.

So, forgive me if I wondered how feed corn could afford the mortgage, or the rent. The tourists simply cannot buy all that much corn, and they have a dizzying selection of road side shacks they can choose to buy from; and, separately, the feed corn bulk market requires numbers bigger than you can grow in a townhouse. That is math. Nothing but math. It isn't about feed corn moving in next door. I am happy to have earthy, earth-bound neighbors. It is the uppity invaders I cannot stand. It was not so long ago I was blue collar myself. I'm happy to see practical produce, and to wish that it prospers; but I just do not get the numbers.

From my second story back window I can peer over our shared privacy fence and catch them flat-leaved in their tiny backyard. For hours, they will stand there, all at attention, slowly following the sun. I admit: the whole of it fascinates me. When the weather allows, on damp days I will open my window just to hear the rain gently speckle their long, loping leaves. I have always been comforted by that sound. It takes a much harder rain to make that soft, soothing sound into an angry, disturbing noise - a threat that nonetheless leaves nourishment puddling on the concrete.

I have never had much interaction with them. There is little in common between a stand of corn and a manager at a shoe emporium. They are usually out in back most mornings when I leave for work; and are inside, surely under heat lamps and green grow bulbs, by the time I slip back into my driveway. I have bought corn at the farmers markets - even feed corn can be quite good when brought home fresh and immediately boiled in salted water - and I have consumed far too much casual corn syrup; but it is hard to have a relationship with corn before it is harvested. I am no farmer. I do not know the day to day travail of corn; nor its idiosyncrasies; nor its loves; nor what motivation it has for any of its incidental pleasures.

But I continue to wonder how simple, unadorned feed corn could afford the townhouse alongside mine. Not an end unit. No fireplace. Only two baths. A privacy fence around the patch of backyard hardly bigger than a family's grave. But how much money can feed corn bring in each month?

This sort of question can work on a man. Townhouse neighborhoods are always on the edge. A bad owner here, a bad tenant there, and suddenly you live in a ghetto. And that worry can prey on a man's sense of self-worth. The health of where you live says a lot about you, about how you have conducted yourself through your past and into your current situation. Too often, it tells your peers everything they need to know. It is no good to let your neighbors get too far behind you, or too far ahead.

So I have been wondering: feed corn?

Much of the recent good weather I have watched the ears next door develop. The shucks have entwined and the silk has draped drunkenly down and the leaves have interlocked and laughed with a full mouth of sun. The stalks grow ever thicker, and I imagine their excess can be harvested for ethanol conversion and thus create yet more income. But I run my simple manager's mathematics and think: not enough.

I have not taken my decision to act lightly, or without sleeplessness, or with no thumping on the bared side of my house listening to the resounding timber of its worth. End units cost more than internal units. This stand of corn house budget mystery goads me. The notknowing sharpens me and spurs into my television time and my pre-sleep preparations, and causes me to ponder whether my station - the level I hold as a home owner, this status that I have achieved in my resident, densely crowded field of consistency - is in fact stable, homogenous, and harmonious. You can see I must resolve this.

I am not one to interfere with the aspirations of my neighbors, but you do understand their aspirations can color my own. None of this is about corn. It is about the right sort of corn.

When some auspicious time is spread out like a trap, I will put a pot on the stove and salt some water. My ladder alongside the common privacy fence, I will wait for the drumming of a dreary, overcast day - a day with the lot of them standing lackluster in their backyard, the season nearly done. All I need is one ear, one ear snatched by stuffing myself half-way up the ladder, reaching a hook arm over the fence, finding an ear by feel or by angling one eye barely above the top of the fence — and making the quick tug that will bring that ear away and over to me.

An ear shucked as I slip down the ladder; silk pulled free and left to the writhing wind as I head for my open back door. The alembic of water, inside, will already be boiling. It takes only a few minutes in the cooking, a few minutes in the cooling. And then, with but one bite: is this the ordinary feed corn I have come to know throughout the magical whirls and swirls and turns of my ordinary life; or is this really, really fancy corn?

YOU MIGHT HAVE TO LEAVE
HOME TO SUCCEED

You don't have to work here long to see everything: everything, at least for a while. You think you are wise. You think you are worldly. You think you have seen everything. Then your very first day on the job you see something so outrageous that you think: now I have seen everything. And then the next absurdity comes along.

It's not like normal bars. Your typical place has a mix of locals, barflies, accidental travelers. Mostly there will be only one or two stray off-worlders: out of place shadows who are probably looking for something, who have some plan, who want more than the drinks and counter food. Some Tellurian will wander into a bar on Nevia, looking at the floor, edging up to the bar like it were going to bite him if he startled it, will order a cold zeeple and, while he's running both hands along the outside of the shivering bottle, under his breath ask where he can find a Nanurian: even though there is a Nanurian flashing six colors just at a table thirteen standard galactic feet away. A Prozoan, struggling with the gravity, will stagger in and tell the bartender this place was on the Registry Of Zamphyte Worship Zones, expecting to extort half price service — and then stay to be overcharged by ten percent. Two BoBabs will come in howling and snapping and scaring all the locals who have never seen a BoBab, outside of the nesting period; they will settle entwined at a table nearest whatever window looks cleanest and order a fisker of gleam, and the bartender will have to ask them for that concoction's perilous ingredients list.

But not here. Here in a corner of the transfer station you get one of just about everything. Barfucates will come in wearing their public suits and order thimble drinks to be poured directly into their access chutes. Razores dejectedly wallow in, sit on the broad benches at the far end of the bar, and spend all night chasing the lumcrawlers scurrying across the counter where I have set them up as free finger food to salt the customers' drinking nodules - and get the greediest chasers buying quart after quart of Zinn Quadrant beer.

Every one of these patrons knows the drill. Each has crawled or stumbled or danced into bars in every way station and transfer point and salvage shop in the galaxy. You don't over charge these customers. And you don't set up too palatial a suite of free food, or pretty the place up too much, or contract for more than one Nanurian: if you do more than the customary, they think you are trying to gain favor with them, they think you have an agenda, they think in the ever watchful bottoms of their brains that there is something they have that you want. Here for a hitch in travel, they seek basic service with basic inebriants and unremarkable finger food at expected prices, and to be a bit less alive when they head out to continue their journey. They want a bit of a stupor, or an hour with the Nanurian, or thirty minutes of suspended animation: and no tentacles whipping across their laps or feathers in their faces or locals pointing and asking what, dear God, is that appendage good for.

The worst I've had here was the time the Phoriphant showed up, walked directly up to the bar and said, "Zeungslatz".

I said, "Excuse me? I don't really know that one, but my pidgin is not all that good so maybe you have another name for it?" I had, up to that time, never seen a Phoriphant, and had no way to guess what he might be asking for, what might fizz his flames, what he might cherish while his life is rolling up at the corners as he awaits the next transport. I'm told Phoriphants don't get out much.

He leaned a little in towards me, like it were some secret, or as though perhaps the name he was going to give me might, by a handful of species, be considered fighting profane, and he said "Zeungslatz!"

As I said, I had never seen one before, and I did not know much about Phoriphants, but that is not unusual. You can't know every species. You learn more and more as you go on, but even by the time you have a few colossal revolutions behind you, there is still always some dark quadrant dweller who collects himself or herself or itself on a bar stool and you look straight through him or her or it, and think: zueth, I hope he, she or it knows what fills the need, because I could not find the need of this thing with a depth finder, two freegeans, and a galactic standard half hour head start.

That being said, I had the best night of my life with a species I had never seen before, after she wandered up to the bar and spent the rest of the night patterning strombo after strombo, and then asked me for an after-hours tour of the station in that sort of voice that said she had no desire for any tour of the station. What a night, and my apartment turned inside out, and the whole of me entirely coiled into happy exhaustion: at least until morning, when I learned this species is asexual and I might have been manually, so to speak, refilling the bladder on a weak organic balance gyro. With that knowledge, only the exhaustion remained. But I don't think about it.

Phoriphants are pretty solid and take well to a standard atmosphere mix, and this one at first seemed to be getting along just fine and my only worry was whether I could concoct whatever it was he was asking for. I have a lot of ingredients, and all sorts of mixing devices, and a few empatheters, as well as about every steady state molecular injection system ever made; but sometimes the task is simply a lentil too far.

I noticed then that this Phoriphant was at that moment about twenty percent bigger than when he had first walked in. That is always bad. That is one of the two or three things you do not like to see, even if it might be normal for the species at hand. Nothing good typically comes of it, whether it is emotional, chemical, sexual or gravitational. A lot of species change size, but typically not in a bar when placing an order. And even in this utilitarian establishment, there are breakable things about: particularly when a solid block of lead by some species is a breakable item. I didn't want to be rude, but I suspected I could not wait long, so I hit the environment hazard button. Thank Loris the alarms have been silent ones for years. No general panic. But by the time the two Guardians slung around the access portal, and with their truck got behind him, the Phoriphant was nearly fifty percent bigger than when he came in and I was screaming at the unlistening, workmanlike Guardians "I didn't serve him anything! Not a sip, not a taste, not a smell! I gave him nothing!"

As one of the Guardians tipped the Phoriphant back onto the truck's tractor feed, the Phoriphant said, "Zeungslatz! Zeungslatz!", waving three of his short arms as though to swim; and the other Guardian cautiously said to no one in particular, but perhaps to me in general, "Her"; and just as the shield slapped down behind the, by then, gutturally expletive - I think - grumbling Phoriphant, we all heard the explosion and it seemed even the station rocked: and I thought for a minute there would be a hole drilled somewhere and the atmosphere would start leaking and we would all be in life support bubbles, with the strobe bursting and the sirens gurgling and the tracer mist coming down in fathoms, and each of us privately left with only what we could grab nearby in the half second before gel.

That is what you think when you've never seen a Phoriphant shed. They usually can time it around their travels, but every so often they go into a molt right in the middle of a long trip, or a delay punts them off cycle, and they have to let fly wherever they are. Like this one, they will try to get to the nearest official and request a pressure chamber, but I did not know what he - well, she - was asking, or demanding, or warning me about. Of course, that was then. I know now. I keep an eye on Phoriphants. Actually a quite pleasant species, if you care for that sort of thing.

Next day, having had to delay her transfer, she was back in the bar, a third of her original size, stuffing into her feeder slits a plate of barely toasted zuches like it was a last meal, and tilting back fisker after fisker of lamentine.

You would never have that happen tending bar in the industrial section of a small rock circling a half burnt out sun, or taming your manners in an inner city smut palace serving contraband scintles to uppity power brokers who tip you a day's salary for your being fulfilled in their service. Out here, you get to see it all. Out here, you are providing something and getting something, and things happen that keep you tethered in your own skin like a clutch of maribunds in the atmosphere of Jupiter.

I keep moving. Looking busy makes busy. The place is never really crowded, but the key to financial success is that there is always someone coming through. The transports run on a highly choreographed schedule, maximizing the use of the facility's support structure and staff, and keeping a fairly consistent number of entities milling through the public areas. The only bad times are when you get a run of clientele that can't take the mix of atmosphere standard enough to support most species: and those end up staying pretty much to the lower decks in un-serviced comfort bins, counting their change, or grooming, or tapping latency theory on the walls as they wait for the next hop unit in their travel itineraries to arrive, get fueled, get cleaned, get blessed and get back on the rails to get shot into the physics of interstellar traffic. But those bad times don't last, and there are relatively few of that kind taking up market share in the galactic travel trade, and so I can expect business in just about every slot of the time bucket.

What more can you want? A customer base that spends, if not much, consistently, that has no hidden agenda, and which has to be out before they overstay their welcome? So the light out here is artificial and the air grown only to adolescence and the food synthesized. I can get a hop to a planet if I want it. I can clip into my savings and get a stationkeeper discount ticket to any of the great, crowded city worlds; or I can decide to toast my cheedas alone on a dull and silent-as-BoBab-eggs agricultural outpost, where the beauty is so sharp it can cut through exposed skin like the Zuxic atmosphere. My neighbors come and go. Which is generally a good thing. I don't have to worry about the Nanurian I am dating imprinting on someone else and starting to rent out her connection ports in any other name than mine. I have a domestic routine, and I am happy sticking to the ceiling of my private apartment.

I have a place as a service agent. I get to complain to station management. I sit in on the planning meetings. I get to argue the priority on my shipments. My parents never thought that I, a simple Prince of Chicago, would get to manage my own bar, and to do so in a transport station besotted with a thousand species, all carrying standard galactic currency credit cards. They thought at first I should stay at home, study the holes in inter-galactic flight theory, or get one of those basement jobs in tech manual illustration.

No. Stations like this are a small democracy. And, at the end of the day, the administrators wander in, ask me if I've developed any new concoctions; quiz me on what is selling and the time-bucket patterns around the purchases for specific product brands; ask if my Nanurian girlfriend, George, is flashing in lusciously repeatable patterns today; or if I have been able to get over the smell of that Mallafed who had the small tear in his suit, which he never noticed, but which nearly killed everyone around him.

I lean back, the contact magnets on my skin suit clacking and cracking. I have a place here. I have a cast of characters who depend upon me. I look out at the Universe and know that coming in tomorrow could be anyone and anything from anyplace out there, and I get to try to make them happy. I get to try to make them forget who they are and where they are going. Do you get the opportunity to do the Universe such service?

Along with being a purveyor, in one way or another, of finger food, sex, alcohol and body odor, I am a cure for the galaxy's social and private boredoms. A galaxy's gift to itself. Maybe a part of the Universe's great happiness conveyor belt. And it pays well.

SHEEP

You possibly find it strange, but an understanding of the mechanics insuring my failure with my first profession, provided the betting-man's impetus for the booming success of my current profession. In that early profession, I had, during twenty-eight years, produced three books, the latest of which at the time of my awakening was new to the public and, without much notice, seeking a home with a wildly disinterested citizenry. Grand fame and recognition were never on the horizon, but I had hoped for some small ripples in the glittering toilet bowls of the literati. Yet, nothing. Nothing at all. No adoring fans, no sales; nothing but dark beyond the glaring edge of the barely audible dribble of an occasional embarrassed royalty check.

One night, curling about the cheap wine that is obligatory to those saddled with aspirations similar to my own, I observed that this year more Americans will have sex with sheep than will buy my book.

Sadly, for both the sheep and me, it is true. As a starkly feathering statistic, more anonymous sheep in this stoically spread out year will get romanced by my fellow countrymen than, amongst those same selective countrymen, copies of my book will be sold.

I do not take it personally. There are books sold in numbers greater than sheep are violated, but by a relatively small number out of the clipped mass of authors frolicking about in our fickle world of publishing; and only books on a relatively few topics - such as pornography or the joys of serial incest or histories written from the new point of the newly imagined victor - do endlessly well. Yes, some authors produce bad work. But often it is not the fault of the authors. Often it is not the fault of the marketers. Consider: have you seen prime time television? Have you wondered who a Kardashian is sleeping with tonight? Have you gotten excited over whether this is the week Wild Man gets his bath?

Over the strikingly clear days after I made my claim of statistical loss, I reconsidered my observation, and checked the numbers. You have to state your queries very carefully to get at the truth beneath any bland, simple, morose data collection on subjects such as these.

Then I decided: why not?

I put a mortgage on the house, dipped into my small savings, and set myself to proving I could be practical. I opened a small shop in an abandoned space that had been a mini-mart once popular with the construction workers - until the big housing development nearby ate up all the land it was allotted and the construction workers migrated. It sat back in a brooding dark spot in a small, comfortable strip mall: gray and deceptively elfin and monstrously squat and ragingly unremarkable.

I did not expect that early on, most of my customers would be locals: recent immigrants and longtime multi-generation-born-and-bred residents, all of whom intended a more epicurean than erotic use for their sheep purchases. They would come into the shop bent on business, in family groups, looking for non-existent scales, and bringing simple ropes. They could have gone to local shepherds, driven out to the greenbelt that girds our small urban and depressing suburban core; but my shop is convenient, it is in town, and I take credit cards.

These sheep I had selected myself, bathed, whitewashed, even festooned with ribbons along their backs and foreheads. I cringed to know what use they would be put to, imagining the quick ends and the mechanical sputter of a backyard grill; but I had to make my living.

For a while, it was as unsettling as watching the sales of my latest book hover unwanted and without purpose, like anonymous trash on the face of someone else's swimming pool. I had even named some of the sheep.

At the lowest depths of my depression, I started to wonder if morally I could accept the unintended outcome of my fledgling business; but business was going not so badly. Customers returned. I had a profit margin, and I began to feel justified in letting an imagined ignorance of my product's final demise casually consume me.

Soon, however, I noticed a happy change in the character of my clientele. More nervous, distracted men - sometimes dressed in raincoats or unneeded overcoats - would show up alone, diluting the number of those large families that swirled in and poked and prodded the sheep: the earthy families looking only for meat potential. These new customers - slowly angling sideways into my shop, tipping forward their hats, sliding down in their unnecessary topcoats - would look over the sheep, have me turn the potential purchase one way or another, and then back. They would stroke the animal's withers, and finger the wool along the animal's side. They would ask me to walk the sheep around the aisles, and ask to see the sheep's feet, inquire about the health of the sheep's gums. After the inspection and interrogation, a sale was quick, and an exit quiet.

I reinvested my profits, and had the front of my building painted pink. I had some decorative plants placed at the curb, to project the face of my storefront further out into the main line of the shopping mall. My lease holder remarked the increase in traffic, opined that all the tenants of the strip mall were feeling the improvements my shop was making. In front of my newly bright business, he gestured with a sloping hand across the great bounty of his real estate. He was open to my suggestion that he move the news stand brooding on my shop's right side, and let me put in a grooming salon. In the early days, there was no need for it: sheep leaving my shop would not be back, and I prepared my product in the small back room next to my unloading dock: I used a child's wading pool, a hose, and occasional spray glitter. But the character of my customer was changing, and I was beginning to see the strength of the statistics I had found. I could customize my product. The landlord could taste at least the edge of my vision, grasp the mathematics I was driving my future with.

With a boutique, I could hire a professional to whitewash the sheep, custom cut coats, clean teeth, and wick creative with ribbons and bows and strings of foil. People, who bought sheep for relation-ships longer than a single-meal, could return with their beloved other-species family members for touchup and beautification, for professional bathing, and an individualized deep shearing.

As the months progressed, couples began to come in, and the market marginally changed again. I dyed a few of my sheep, and sold them with the names I had long playfully created for them. Oh, there was still the occasional brute of a man who showed up, selected the smallest and most ordinary of sheep in the shop, paid cash, and carried the startled animal out to the back of his truck. Families who saw nothing but sustenance in our transactions still patronized me, all but carrying tableware. Young college students still arrived in oversized raincoats. But more often there would be a well-dressed couple, each individual reaching out to scratch the sheep between the ears, to look in the animal's comforted eyes, to feel about the healthy belly and to exult at the small, utterly meaningless vocalizations the sheep would make.

I took the retail space on the left of my main store, turning it into a customized lingerie shop. I carry fishnet stockings shorter than you can find anywhere else. I stock garter belts with a ninety degree dip. I display leashes of the softest leather; tethers and restraints made of calf's hide, made even of ostrich feathers.

I spend my time researching new accoutrements, the latest styles in shearing, trends in tastes. A while ago, I even put in a book section. You would be surprised how many books there are on the scintillating joys of cross-species sex. For individuals. For couples. For groups. I put in two thick shelves of pure print to go with a thin shelf of video.

I can finally feel comfortable in my success. I have a total seven thousand square feet of retail floor space, four employees, and three local suppliers. I became a member of the retail merchants association. I get half a pound of marketing junk mail each day. I know when I arrive at my shop each morning that there will be recognizing and welcoming bleats from the handsome stalls where my in-stock wares have been resting overnight.

Yet, there is still an old pull, a deep lust for communication; and at times I stealthily retire unknown to the back den of my home, curling in on my secret activities like clipped feathery sheep shearings on the floor: to write. Quietly, with the desk light pulled low and the draperies closed, I fold over my notebook and try to call up the enthusiasm of my misspent, unprofitable, unsophisticated earlier years. I let no one know, and the few pieces I send out to the still hopeful, though never read, small and unheralded literary markets, I do so under an obscure and unfathomable pseudonym. In polite company, writing for the literary market is not pristinely unheard of; but it is not something one brags about. Your neighbors mention it at a party only if they are trying to get you to leave. Sheepishly, you would admit to it only if you wished to be a public pariah. And those of your closest intimates - those who know that this inane scribbling is how you selfishly, with improbable joy and meaningless accomplishment, express yourself - recoil silently, and allow in the most forgiving parts of their hearts that there is room in this world for all manner of strange, unholy, and pointless things: perhaps.

But not even they believe that lie; not even as they look into your sad-while-happy, emptying eyes and think: what might there be behind those eyes that could cause him to shamelessly take up pen and paper and wander purposefully so far away from the light?

In ways, I am glad that all the public needs in its literature is the rough outline of want -and a doleful, uncomprehending, yet blissfully apprehensive, bleat. And thankful that I can rely on my presentable business to keep me from revealing my brazenly unpardonable one.

SHEPHERDS

The children settle into the truck, comfortable with sliding together along the ripped and battered seat until they knock their hollow shoulders. None appears happy, but none creates the sort of survival fuss and confusion Hank expected. To Hank, they seem to be stuck in neutral, not even grinding gears.

Mixed in no particular order, the children range in age from perhaps eight to twelve, except for one gossamer phantom shape of a girl Hank calls 'Mina'. He does not know her real name. He could ask Lenny, but Lenny would just make something up, spit out the most challenging gutturals of the local language, or coin a term that in the native tongue would be an outhouse joke. You can love Lenny, as long as you don't trust him.

Mina is possibly thirteen, maybe a precocious twelve, but easily the oldest of the bunch. If Hank scolds his imagination really, really hard, he might see her as fourteen: or at least at the heavy end of a year younger, and about to turn. When Hank first saw her, his glossy, well-thumbed memories of what he had expected resigned themselves to revision; and Mina became what he had expected that she, in the peaks of his ungainly thrills before he arrived, would curiously be.

None of the gathered children's ages are known by either Hank or Lenny. No one asks. No one asks anything. This is the first time Hank has come collecting with Lenny, and he is amazed at the steel-toothed business manner locked into the whole of it.

Lenny knows what he is looking for. The village knows what Lenny is looking for. He has been to nearby villages and the word has spread. The crop has been culled in advance, and he takes nearly every child offered. There are too many boys, so three he turns back. In his harvest he has mostly girls, and a wider age range of those. The boys don't seem to show any above ten. But no one knows the ages. No one asks.

For an exchange that is done openly in the dreary main street of the village, there is a lot of secrecy kept aside for the price. Lenny is careful not to let each family see what he pays for any child, other than for their own. He places his back against the crowd and curls the most of him in towards the selling family, folding over in his fingers his handful of cash, folding like a spider curling up in the sun. Lenny wants to get the best for the least. If the families can peg a value to a given grade of child, the cost for all of the children will go up. After the sale, what they boast they held out for will not matter; but, during the sale, Lenny cannot let them know how high he is willing to go.

"Lenny, this isn't right."

"Hank, you wanted to come."

Hank straightens and turns to look at the spot between Mina's chartless eyes. She has those deep, dark space eyes that seem to drop inward like a gravity well: dropping into exotic and quarantined worlds not even she knows are waiting there. She looks back at him, but seems to peer through him, looking at the field of space around him, or the emptiness behind.

"I know. I wish I hadn't come."

"Hank, what do you think I am doing here? Why do you think I drive out to these one watering-hole, backhand nowheres? These people have so many children they don't know what to do with them. Look around. Children stacked on children. Every other woman is a Mother Hubbard. Vaccines, better sanitation, global do-gooders: once, these villagers would each have ten children, and end up with four to work the family field. Now, they have ten and end up with eight to feed. I take this one away, and his brother tomorrow has enough to eat; I take that one away, and he isn't competing with grandpa for last night's leftover cattle dung soup. I take two away and one of the ones too lanky to sell goes to school."

"I know, Lenny, I know. I've worked out here and I've seen the poverty. These people are a two year drought away from starvation.

Maybe a one year drought. It would be better if we stuffed birth control pills in the relief aid, or neutered them all."

Hank runs an excited, confused eye over the scruff land that seems to be leaning towards making a dust storm of itself. Pack animals look like strays. Herds look like idle individuals passing. The buildings where an entire clan of people once would come together, in the beginning, to erect, seem to barely grip the earth, ready to slip onto their sides and expire in the unfathomable sun.

"Can't do that Hank. The State would be offended." Lenny was looking out over the remaining wares, hoping perhaps to see some that might fit a purpose in demand further inland.

"And this doesn't bother them?" Hank could only look at Mina for so long. Now he was focusing on the grill of the truck.

"You plant flowers around the stench, and the stink of it the State can bear. Or you say you plan to plant flowers, and the State will put up with the stench. Spread a little money around, and they kind of grow to like the smell."

"I say damn the State and cut off the supply chain."

"Don't say that. I'd be out of a job." Lenny looks to prove to Hank the point is to be taken as the proud hammer strike that breaks the moment back to what it is meant to be. He is proud of the levity.

Lenny pushes a rail of a girl up into the truck, Hank catching her instinctively from the other side. Mechanically, she sits on the one bench and slides, like she were being packed into a shipping crate, against the much taller Mina. Hank watches as the two girls crumple easily together, like tissues in the hand of a man about to sneeze. They must recognize each other, but Hank does not see the recognition.

"But what about the children?"

"Hank, think it through. How many, if we left all of them here, would make it? These girls start spitting out children as soon as they bleed, and the boys start learning the trade their family has been stuck with for six centuries. Maybe one, maybe two out of each family walks six miles to school. You do the math. You figure the odds."

"You know what happens to these children."

Hank is looking past Lenny's shoulder, watching two boys not much older than the ones on the truck herding goats. Not really a herd:

more like a chance encounter. And not exactly herding. They seem to be shuffling the goats one way and then back, pounding the ground with fleshy sticks, using the animals like shuttlecocks in a game. The animals startle and rear a little, then move towards one boy, who, as the herd slows, pounds the ground and turns them back to the first. One goat has separated himself from the small pack and is making ever shorter journeys between the boys, letting the pack out pace him. Hank can see the little understanding left in the goat beginning to shrink elegantly smaller and smaller, and Hank knows that in a moment or two it will be small enough and tight enough to be completely wrapped in the animal's doubt: and movement will stop. The animal will, in his own goat schemes and goat beliefs, know that he is only a feature in the landscape of the children's game: a piece set loose, meeting the game's limits, and saddled with the rules made up between the children and the game; that what he, the goat, might do means nothing, and nothing is wanted of him. He is the nearest available game piece.

"No, I don't. I know the family gets out of me as much as a year's wages, one less mouth to feed, and has the opportunity to climb one more rung out of this septic pit. Look at the children. You don't think they are better off working as maids in a house that can afford to feed them, or learning a trade in a factory? All I know is that one hundred fifty miles that way," and he actually turns east and points with one outstretched finger on which the nail has stubbornly split, "I slow at the corner just inside the main city roundabout and a man passes me the address of the warehouse where I drop my cargo. He does a quick count and he is gone. He phones ahead the numbers, I guess. Maybe he is really fast and he runs them in. I do not know. I drive in, unload, and drive out with my empty truck, but now with a little envelope warm in the passenger seat."

"And you won't count it till you clear the warehouse doors."

"Damn straight."

Two of the families whose boys have been refused are standing just a few yards off. Both boys have the same head down, shamed look as the children in the truck. To Hank, it looks like some default they all slip into when they have nothing nearby worth the wetness of eye to look at.

"The morality of it doesn't bother you, eh? You don't want to know where this actually ends? You would rather have the tourist brochure edition?"

Beyond Lenny's shoulder, the goat has stopped. The remainder of the thin herd lazily moves between the two boys, slower than ever, but still moving: mechanically, routinely, shuddering with a learned indifference at each child's angry gestures. This one goat simply stands stock paralyzed, no matter how wild the threat. One of the boys sets to beating the goat, but still it stands. The flails raise dust from the hide, but cannot bite through to blood. The animal looks like an idol constructed of reed and wood set up to be sacrificed to ensure the wealth of the herd, the unlikely milk, the fatless meat. His dingy, dust ridden head hangs with gravity alone. He seems to be breathing no quicker, no deeper, than if he were grazing the peaceful, green fields of Scotland. The tail has forgotten what it is connected to.

The goat is broken. Not as in made tame, but as in no longer functioning like a goat, or like anything: no longer functioning. It is eating its shadow.

"Does a man selling corn to an ethanol plant worry that the price of corn is going to go up for people on the margin in the third, fourth, eighth, or eighteenth world? You can make ethanol out of ragweed. People starve to level out the price of gasoline. Maybe you get real ecological and you go completely to ethanol and the corn sellers still keep their corner of the market and millions starve or have to sell some of their children to buy food for the other children. Morality is a funny thing. I've slept with morality and you would be surprised the tricks it has picked up over the years. It can circle around behind you, come back wearing heels and a thong, with a sexy little whip, and whack you dumbstruck on the back of your unhinged balls."

Lenny and Hank have stopped loading the truck, and Lenny picks up his beaten metal cash box. It will ride on the worn front seat between the two of them, until Lenny puts Hank off about two thirds of the way to the warehouse district at the port. A fork in the road, where Hank had driven that morning to meet his drinking partner and general tag-along in crime: Lenny, the all-around ex-pat handy man.

"Yes, but it is different when you look at the children."

"Yeah. Look at their parents and see how many you have to add together to get a full set of teeth. Look at how many you would say were seventy going on near dead when in fact they are only forty. And going on near dead. The children? Any place with better food, rudimentary environmental controls. Maybe reading, writing and arithmetic. Maybe something better than six weeks of schooling. Maybe something short of staring at the clouds to see if they can catch the difference between rain and starvation. My business ends with it at the warehouse."

Lenny knew. His broad hands murmured of the knowledge. No good end for any of these children, no matter how you cut it. They were all short-changed from the start. No happy ending any place. Except with Mina. Mina would do well for herself. Hank has always had a hunger for that long, straight, scurrilously black hair. For the narrow set shoulders that drifted into the cool smoothness of un-cornered arms. And those eyes that sink so far that a man could climb whole into one painfully sensuous pupil, fall with the freedom of his years retelling their histories differently, and find himself rekindled anew at the bottom.

The girl sits as still as a rock face carved by millennia of glaciers, the hair disappearing teasingly down her back, crushed against the side of the truck. For the moment, she is one of the children selected. She may be two inches taller, a few months older, with eyes that sing shaman songs to Hank, but she is selected.

For Mina alone, Hank has come on this out-of-his-element trip: for someone who would become Mina, for someone who could be believed into being Mina. This is not the sort of place Hank is comfortable. He can know what happens here without witnessing it. He can know it and think whatever he likes, until he witnesses it. And then he has to know.

Mina will leave the truck when Hank leaves the truck. He will slide out with a nod to Lenny, his face still forward to miss the demeanor of the man he has traveled this great distance with. He will motion her out of the truck, pointing and gesturing until she understands; and she will without challenge follow him, becoming quickly the slithering enchantress of his battered car's front seat, as they cut across the open country half-roads to Home. Her depthless, cold purity will be the new spark of his lately withering life, the object into which he might pour all of his ferocious loneliness, his dim revenge for making of himself a man alone in a loveless country.

Hank picks one leg from the passenger seat by pointing his toe on the floor board, the blood edging back from where it had begun to abandon his thigh, and his mind pitching images of his boxed-in future changing in hesitant, delicate steps from dark to light. In the echoes of his imagination he is thinking: damn Lenny; damn him and all the soul-slandering hope he brings. And his imagination is also thinking: for a while, I can be whole again.

THE DISAPPEARANCE

We had not seen these things, and so had to be convinced of their utility. All mothers stagger their babies on their hips, or wear them cradled in front, sometimes cradled in back. But these things: a seat with wheels, and long handles so the mother is always impudently upright: we did not know what they might do, what gain they could give us for the loss of our accustomed intimacy, mother to child.

A government worker, the same one who brought us make-up in sticks and jars and talked about how a woman could say no to her husband, brought them with her in the back of a government pick up truck. With all the banging and leaps of a truck crossing open plain, the devices must be sturdy. We would have suspected that, as with most of what the government people bring us, in a few miles the official gifts would have been piles of wheels and slashed canvass and bent poles. But some thoughtful man stacked these correctly long before he let the woman drive them here. She passed them hand to hand off the truck one at a time, and we stepped up to the tailgate, each taking the offered contraption, even the women who had no children: poor pasty wives - they had no more idea at first than did we for what they might need these curious conveyances.

They are not hard to learn. The baby goes in the seat. The safety strap goes around the baby and buckles. The wheels turn, or slide in the dirt once they are jammed, and it all goes forward with the mother pushing from behind. It could not be simpler. The baby and the mother are now a separate thing. The mother looks down to see the captured baby; the baby looks forward at an onrushing world, and there is no mother.

In time we did see the good side to these. Balancing a baby requires the surrender of one hand. A baby in a sling pulls at the contortions of the back, or simply gets in the way of necessary work, idle play. With the child strapped into the carrier, a woman can use both hands, can keep her hips under her, can go about the workday as though she has no child at all. More often than not, the power of the device is in parking the baby. The mother pushes the baby far enough from home that she does not feel she has to make it comfortable, then leaves it strapped into the mothering device while nearby she might have hands and hips and full motion to apply to whatever desire is at view.

Not a few men have been cuckolded while their children slept bent double in the government stroller, and the wife made comparisons with another woman's husband. With a little technology, there is often a new liberation.

Once the devices were accepted, they began to have their own niche in our elastic culture. People who had no children would put their pets in the strollers and parade about the village, no less proud than a mother of triplets. Some would pile their clothes into the carriers, take them down to the one washing machine available in the village. Some were even pushed empty. At times there would be more women with empty conveyances than filled, each in their finest whoring clothes pushing their cargo of air with an exaggeration that would set the men to howl, these bat-eyed women saying: see, you can fill this.

Then, one woman lashed two carriages together and made a wider one. Somehow she tied them at the frame, kept the wheels independent, made three upright handles out of four. She carried a child on one side, the child's moon bear doll on the other. When she came through the narrower village streets, people would have to pass her single-file. Barely could her double stroller share the road with an opposing single stroller. People looked ahead to see her coming and plotted how to resolve the bristling encounter. She pushed like a musk ox in rut and her smile, close lipped and predatory, warbled of privilege.

Such an effrontery does not last for long. Within the week, a long thin, reed of a woman, with no children at all, and a husband who would travel regularly to other women's beds almost as though servicing a route, lashed three of the devices together. In one seat she would keep her spare sandals; in another she would place a water jug; in the third were the part of her husband's clothes he was not just then wearing. She had to run a stick through the six gregarious handles, and when pushing she could not well keep a straight line. But no matter: she took up the width of most streets, and in the larger thoroughfares stood out as something that simply had to be gotten around.

Other women began to fashion these combined carriages. Some would stop at two, unable to trick more from the government representative. Others would buy the strollers from villagers who were too thick yet to master the need for them, and preferred to balance a child on the hip or in a sling. Oh yes: as though the strategy of strollers was about children. They would quietly bid out the device given them by the government representative, and amongst a small amen group come to the best price and pass ownership, with no thought to the status they were betraying.

For a while, having one was poverty, two strung together was the norm, and three lashed into a unit was the height of fashion. Woman would push the devices at one another, chase men off the road. Their backs would groan as they would plot a line directly through the ambient traffic and then try to hold it as they drove with their legs, steered with the grandeur of their arms, leaned left and right and squatted to bring the best of the rump into the gathering momentum.

But one day, a woman in some unfathomably magical way lashed four together. The consortium was wider than she was tall, heavier than a boy just beyond puberty. Haltingly, she made one round through the main square, the only place a child hauler four carriers wide would fit. She puffed and twisted and could not control the trajectory of her device for the most part, but it moved. It moved. And everyone got out of the way.

From the houses surrounding the square and from the street itself other women watched, some unselfconsciously bending and cackling, trying to get a look at how it was done, how the four devices were effectively held together. There was little control in the driving, and only a monster of a woman could push such a behemoth, but it was astounding, a device that could not make it down most of the village's small paths, that could go round and round the square for as long as a robust winter woman had the strength to push it.

Certainly it was magnificent, but at the same time it was a socializing mystery: how had it been constructed? What was the secret of its unanimity? No one admits to being able to discern it that day. People would describe what they had seen, draw crude engineering guesses in the dust behind their houses. They would turn their own carriages up and down and lay them sideways on their floors and look for strengths that were not there, construction tolerances that did not seem to exist. Soon, they would simply fall to describing again to each other how the woman huffed and threw out her arms and how her huge legs quivered and spoke. They would imagine what she revealed to her husband as she labored on the new species of device, and how he might have busied himself as she measured and fashioned and tested her secret patents in the dark.

She has not been seen since that day. Her glorious hours came and went and no one remembers what she did when she had finished this once only parade. She became, in those short turns of her contraption, mythical. Everyone knows everyone else in this village, cousins marry cousins, and we share one blood: but we do not speak the name of the woman. The government representative can tell us nothing; but remembers the woman as a beast of burden, one who could push four carriages where perhaps none other could. Her husband would have no trouble picking her out in a crowd. He has been seen, alone, snarling at flies thinking to conquer his porch. But he has not seen his wife, or he is not admitting to it. Girls not yet of marrying age, but growing close, parade wiggling by his house, and he looks at them with the snake slit eyes of a man who has not felt the inside of a woman for some time, with the eyes of a mathematician of family lines.

I suspect we shall not see this woman for a while. And I think that soon enough we will find loose wheels and torn canvas and bent tubes that once were handles lashed into a foursome, all in a pile, with the righteous fingerprints of many citizens crawling proudly over the wreckage. The rains will rust it and the winds rip it, and in a generation it will be covered in rot and even the woman's daughter one day will push her own limb-poor daughter in a fashionable, for that day, stroller past the unrecognized rubbish mound. The granddaughter, stumbling indulgently unbuckled from her engulfing stroller and playing on drowsy legs hide-and-seek with her imaginary playmates, might pull at an unintentionally found, scarred, deep-bitten carriage wheel of a style long left to rumored ancestors, and ask over her shoulder, "Mother, what is this?"

And the mother, bending down to be all face and dread, will say, "Why, child, this was your grandmother's. She plowed behind it like an ox on a tether. And either it killed her, or we did."

THE SPECIAL

He bought the horse for his glaringly mediocre daughter: a fine quarter horse, pure-bred, and with papers and a lineage that could be respectably played out in long hand and framed. Everyone knew he paid more for it than some locals had put into their primary family cars. Fourteen hands, it had the look of well-cured, old royalty; with a way of turning its head that dismissed onlookers, no matter how distant they might be. He had a flick of his mane that curried butter, and a gravity that made you respect the grateful air around him.

The whole town knew it was too much horse for the girl. You can't stuff a thousand pounds of proud promise into a hundred pounds of edge-wise sassy. The girl was just not made for a show horse. She folded like a poor man's wallet, and the line of her was a geometry that made sense to average boys. Her slick sided jeans were made for slipping off under the football stadium bleachers, not bearing the subtle pressure that brings a fine equine around to a human sense of direction.

Nonetheless, the man loved that horse. He carried it everywhere he went, and people marveled at it, stood in line to stroke its withers, to look up into its falling-away eyes. The horse would wait patiently on the man's shoulders, balanced with all four legs in the air, drinking in the attention of townspeople and visitors alike, expecting along every inch of himself to be desired and envied. He seemed to understand his public fame, and rested calmly in the place adoration had made for him. Sometimes he would be over the left shoulder, sometimes the right, and occasionally draped placidly around the man's neck. He would hang with luxurious patience, hooves nearly touching the ground - but not quite - and his wondrous legs dangled delightfully down, as straight as a courting boy's sex, and as equally unused.

No one could understand the balance. Yes, the man was larger than most townspeople, but not so large as to make the horse an easy heft. It was thought that only the grace and peerless agility of the horse allowed the man to keep him aloft. Surely, the man had strength and talent, but it was the horse that completed the circle — the horse: whose long, luxurious and pure bloodline made its subtlety and grace an embedded, biological effect of its selective cause. Only in such noble blood would there be the ability to remain in equilibrium, to become with the man one unparalleled balancing unit: a magnificent horse, suspended in the air by a more fragile being, a supporting being of less regal elements, a being without such a panorama of possibilities that such a peerless horse, as this archetypical creation in look and bearing, must have.

The man would walk into town with the horse, tilt the horse with one hand to best advantage on his shoulders, and still have one hand to use in greeting, or opening doors for strangers, or carrying his purchases. When he had to go into a building, he would carefully set the horse down, and the horse would stand there waiting while the man busied himself inside: the horse waiting with his head up, waiting without obviously being either waiting or not waiting, yet still being the center of attention. When the man's business was done and he came back out, the man would lean sideways into the horse, reach around under his belly, shimmy his knees, and drive the horse up. I have seen him do it with half a week's groceries towed in a sack in his other hand. The horse remained stone faced throughout.

This town is not so rich as to not be mindful of which stray bits and pieces of ordinary life might be turned into profit. Soon, the local businessmen's club decided to print up flyers, and to impress them at the bigger towns along the road leading uncertainly here. People would want to see the fine horse, held aloft by the man who bought him and loves him and carries him everywhere. Visitors need a reason to come visit. This wondrous horse could be a reason. Restaurants and Five and Dime stores could, it was proposed, harvest the unsuspecting gawkers; hot dog carts could call ahead to find out where the man might be going that day and strategically place themselves in advance, parking where unsuspecting voyeurs might linger. People attempting to measure the horse - to harvest some of the nobility of that noble horse, to mark how the man is ennobled by such a burden - would be rife for the street vendors, the small store fronts, and even the larger establishments proudly displaying sidewalk hurdy-gurdies.

We would honor the horse, and be sustained by the return on the depth of our appreciation.

Our venture worked marvelously. People came, and the man walked through town and the horse looked regally past everyone, staring out of the lower half of his eyes, dropping his business when he felt like it, the extra height focusing gravity and making for a remarkable thud, and on special occasions a splatter. The man carried the horse at home as well, and some guests drove out to his place, parked street-side to wait for the man, just in case he decided to come out, pick up the horse that was left idle by the working class entry back door of the middle class farmette home: and then stride about the yard, or carry the special animal to the drab barn. One man would walk along the street, hawking coffee and treats, feeding the waiting congregation from a stash of day old brew and week old pastries that otherwise would go to waste.

I suspect the man nearly stank of pride in that horse. He had chosen a good companion. We all thought better of the man for his excellent choice in horses. His family became the object of speculation. Was the man so gifted at selecting other opportunities, other creations as well? The caliber of men and boys seeking to date his daughter markedly improved, and the scenery where she became their working flesh saw an up tick in class and refinement: with her entire experience of each carnal event having a more appreciative and longer lead in; and being speckled with more patternless small talk, more follow through, and an occasional repeat performance.

Our luck would not hold out forever. We do not know how old the horse was when the man bought him, but by the time the man's daughter had saddled her second husband, the horse was surely old, and though happy to be carried, nonetheless was approaching his expected expiration. And then one day he died. We do not know what of. Maybe a ruptured spleen or some malady associated with the pressure of a rough shoulder in his belly. One morning the man simply went to the barn to pull out the horse and get him up on his shoulder, to settle him into the groove of his long utility - and the horse was over and gone. All that nobility and regal bearing, that peerless haughtiness and lovingly languid disdain, reduced to horse flesh that would need to be expunged in the usual way. The town was sad and indignant and without answers, each citizen holding on to his now somewhat thinner shadow and feeling as though the special had been spirited out of our lives.

The man was heartbroken. He seemed bent in burden. And he bought three graves across in the municipal cemetery, then started to take donations for a monument. The entire town turned out for the funeral, if only to see the broken man, to watch him pass the hat. But the man still possessed his strength, his drive. And with his daughter no longer of riding age, he could, if he had the will to stagger on, make a selection of horse more appropriate to the use he had in mind for it.

We could not tell in his demeanor what his character would countenance. There was a buzz of it. Old couples would opine on the man's options in the pre-sleep banter that years before would have been the prelude to industrial sex. Concern for the man would be the introductory line in young couples' opening banter before their training sex. One pastor referenced it in a small, cautious corner of his Sunday service.

From two towns over, the man bought a draft horse: a great monster of a beast, noticeably outweighing the original royal equine, and the lifting of which would be some feat. Broad shoulders and thick in the limbs, the working horse would require more blind skill of the man; but better demonstrate his mastery of balance, and of the communication between muscle and bone. It is rumored the animal had hauled barrels at a craft brewery, one of those places that revel in doing business in primitive ways, draft horse and all, as though the primitive alone were in any way ennobling. The horse had pulled a cart or a sled or some other impractical means to accomplish practical ends, and was eventually seen as an economic liability.

On an average day, he hefted the horse, and strode into town and people moved out of his way. The horse sat calmly on his shoulder, head moving side to side, looking always down, eyes always down, his tail swishing the back of the man's neck. The horse would neigh, and occasionally kick, rock forward or backward awkwardly: making the man artfully adjust, swing about in nearly inhuman ways, skillfully arrange himself in rapid and fickle gravities, and contort into geometries almost no other man could accomplish.

The tourists stopped coming. The hot dog vendors returned to the strip outside of the fair grounds. The coffee vendors went back to selling their wares as cheap contraband to children. Locals would nod, but not stop to talk. Everyone was pleasant to the man, but his fame slipped ever quicker away, like the heat of a candle in a cold room, or the wisdom of a man who ceases to learn.

He walked about, and the horse simply hung alternately limp, alternately fidgety, looking like the brute force whose time had passed that this horse truly was. He fouled the street with the end of his digestion; he smelled of sleeping too late in straw that needed to be refreshed. He was the type of horse anyone might see if practical feats of dumb, brute strength had not been turned over to simple, lithe machines.

Poor man. He could not understand this was no longer the same; that the reason for this attempt at art was insufficient. Townspeople began to think he carried a once good thing too far, and muttered as much under their breathing as he strode overburdened through town. His exertions were seen as unnecessary; and even his daughter asked him to stop.

And so he stopped.

And the horse milled about in the open spaces behind the man's house and he survived, thinly, the first winter - the shadow of an opportunity laced into the clothing of a mystery - but not the second. He was put into the earth beyond the edge of the barn and quite possibly on someone else's untended property, the lines sometimes being a bit confused given the inutility of the land. Done and done, before the first good freeze, when the earth would turn too hard and unbreakable for such humility. Done. And so much for that beaten and befuddled man. Perhaps it would have been better had he never learned to balance a horse at all.

THE RIGHTIST

After our visits, my wife is daggers, thorns, steel wool and lye. She is the rough and ire of a gap toothed wood file. I do not care to visit that neighbor's house with her in tow, but one does have to be sociable.

The man is pleasant enough. The three of us can carry a conversation as easily as a bell choir can ring out a scale. We have enough in common that our relationship has symmetry, yet each of us can be safe in our own personal pools of expertise. It is the man's wife who creates my problem. In her tank on the indoor/outdoor wet/dry carpet, she bobs across the length of the glass nearest where my wife and I sit warily, pushing her head above the water to speak or listen more closely. The thin mid-lid of her eyes roll back when she edges out of the damp; and at times she will brace the crook of her arm on the top ledge of her enveloping ten foot by six foot by eight foot aquarium.

What she has to say is no trouble. You can hear, in the background of her practiced voice, the squeal and pop that would be her native tongue; but it has been left with the coral and anemones, and coastal English is her tongue now. She has become quite elegant in the tank, regally balancing against the weight of the water with small and curiously dainty vacillations of her tail. She folds at the hips and leverages the current of the tank's aerator. Her shoulders lead, and she now and again will place her hand flat on the glass, pushing herself into a better study of the world outside.

None of this upsets my wife, and we are all quite engaged with the adaptability and finesse this woman, while relaxed in her tank, can display. If this were all there were to it, I could stand being neighborly. But soon my wife will catch me, as I cannot stop myself, watching the woman languorously draw her huge, bare breasts across the glass of the unsympathetic aquarium, then flatten without mercy those wonderful masses against the restraining clear barrier. I try not to let my mouth drop open, and I look away, at least in small krill-like catches. She hangs there, as though affixed by the confusion of skin on glass, and I shiver, only a little, but too noticeably to someone who has been watching my reactions at nearly the subatomic level since the moment we arrived.

I can feel the lead pipe sternness of my wife's stare foundering ingloriously on the back of my head. She sits deep into the couch and will not be unfolded for any rational purpose. I can see the hair along her arms rise in attention, dry urchin spikes ready to be set, and I can sense along all my intangibles my near term happiness sinking like a fisherman's weight set free of its line.

I cannot help myself. It is not a matter of will. I react like any man. It is not as though I harbor any thought of exchange, of an upgrade, or even of comparing one wife to the other. I have the wife I want, all of her dry and openly mobile. But when this other man's wife kicks with the dazzling perpendicular force of her fluke and flares the full felicity of her magnificent ballast against the love-struck glass, no man could look casually away, no man could tolerate the event without his blood shifting lucklessly out of his brain and into his most precious weapon.

I am not at fault. And I go home, expecting to prove to my turbulent wife that there are no residual images to my widened vision yet lingering - and she covers my best efforts in salt, strands me in the shallows of her imagined second place finish. I reach with both hands, hoping to palm comfort, and they are denied me. I sleep hugging my side of the bed as though it were the last finger of flotation between me and drowning alone.

After months of this, her jealousy continues as fresh as it was with her first rage, with my first unknowing, unavoidable offense. I would prefer the two of us not go to this neighbor's house together. But we are all on good terms, and I do not see why I should let suspicion poison our mutual waters. I am honorable, but my wife acts as though I were but a bottom feeder, ready for anything that might be laid out thoughtlessly before me. I am not, but soon the entire neighborhood will have me guilty simply from the bile and brine my wife exudes over her socially crafty coffee parties.

So I decide I must talk to the man. I must explain my concerns, the trials my wife puts me through, the spot his wife's genius lays on my ordinary life. I must ask him to have the woman house her half that is not scale in some sort of sheath, some bathing suit top, some water friendly vest. She must understand her gift, and keep it close, keep it secret. Or at least keep it out of my marriage.

I knock on his door repeatedly, knowing from the presence of his car that he is home. The door sends ripples through the frame and I begin to knock again. He does not answer at first, but I continue, waves of resolve flowing through me with the force of the slights unjustly sprayed against my husbandly character by my bristling wife. I have captured, for a few moments, my courage and must press the issue. Those wondrous baubles must be properly veiled.

At the last moment of my conviction, he opens the door. Dripping he stands, a towel wrapped about his hips and held in place with a grasp more like a fist in birth than the coil of an effort at stability, his eyes a dull gray and slow to focus. A trail of water leads back into the house, down the hall that lies in open view of the front door, and to the tank; where low in one corner, her hair a net of disharmony in agitated water, the man's wife lies folded over her own fluke, trailing bubbles from the corner of her spent mouth. She peers over her lolling, slightly reddened shoulder at me, and places one hand in half a greeting on the aquarium glass angled nearest my slowly perceiving gaze.

Gathering his own breath in jellyfish snatches, the man distantly, carefully asks what could I possibly want; and only then do I think, for the very first time, of just how back-breakingly small that damn tank is.

BUTTERFLIES

1.

Wonjel listened a moment to her mother busying upstairs, then turned back to watch Nika putting away toys. Nika seemed to enjoy putting away toys more than anything, more than even playing with toys. The small, slightly stooped under-girl whirled about looking for things out of place, and then put them back where they should be with a giggle and a glint of self-satisfaction that Wonjel wondered whether she herself would ever have. Nika maintained a joy in such simple things. Maybe it was not Wonjel's place to have such self-satisfaction.

"Make sure Nika has on her tan tunic", Wonjel's mother called from upstairs, her voice not unpleasant, but knifing through the air. Wonjel's mother was in the throes of what she called 'getting ready', a ritual that preceded any other ritual or occasion. Nika had a tendency to slip off her tunic, but Wonjel almost always made her keep it on when she was in the house.

Wonjel patted down her yellow dress, and glanced at the yellow sash her mother was sure to make her wear. Nika would wear the tan tunic she usually wore. Nika was not of the People. Nika was of the under-species, a class of hominid without the soul of the People, without the gifts for learning and reciting. The People could weave and plant and reap and herd, and reading was becoming popular even amongst the moneyed classes. Poor Nika. Her people dwelt drearily at the edge of the Arid Places and would come, if they were lucky, to be playmates for the People. Nika did not know her own history, and her words were blurt and spit, expression that was discouraged in better company. The under-girl had a face not too unlike her more evolved masters, but her skin was thicker and her mind not of the People's geometry, and her soul seemed to have leaked out long ago.

Surely, Nika understood that there was excitement about today, but she could not know what the excitement itself was for. She luxuriated in the electricity of others, in the spice littering the air: though she had no idea why the electricity was there, why the spice was lingering on the edges of everything. Later, Wonjel would help Nika comb her hair, and would make sure her tunic was on right side up and inside in, centered on her shoulders, and securely clipped on.

2.

I put away the things. I know what is out of place. I know what needs to go back into its place. I see Wonjel be happy and I am happy. Happy Wonjel, happy Nika. I hear the noise of Wonjel's mother, but I do not understand her want. She makes great motions when small ones will do. The sound at times is fearful. I do not fear Wonjel's mother. I had a mother. I do not remember mother. But I do remember clinging, and of being in my place.

Wonjel has a father. I keep away from Wonjel's father. I keep away especially when he is alone. He has the way of claiming things. He is full of anger and invasion and I do not understand how he is made happy. I put away the toys. I use a clumsy device to order my hair. I understand its use when I see it, but when I cannot see it the device becomes dull and without name and sometimes Wonjel helps me. She orders my hair and tames the device and I see myself as Wonjel must see me. It helps Wonjel to help me.

I would want a mother like Wonjel's mother, but without the softness of scent. I would fear a father like Wonjel's. A father of howl. Wonjel's world is more complicated than I have the wonder to waste upon it.

3.

It is the yellow that calms the Whu-ta-k'in. There is something in its radiance. Something in its soothing appeal. It is why the People worship yellow. Why golden hair is a gift from God. Why the roofs of houses are painted yellow. Why paddocks are shielded in yellow. Why the prize breeding stock is outfitted in yellow. Why the People, on the day of the Whu-ta-k'in migration, all stand in yellow and watch as the massive flight comes through and the Phe-butoo are exchanged.

The Whu-ta-k'in can be fierce. The size of two well-formed men, they glide on their butterfly wings, in a swarm of thousands. The sudden beat of their wings can down a small child, can deafen the most gossipy of old women. The creatures gather out of the forests North of the Arid Places, rising up each as one lone ingredient, joining the stream that flies across the Northern forests and the Arid Places and into the land of the People; and then on to cross the uncharmed sea to settle again in the Southern forests where they live, solitary in the season amongst shadows. There they wait for the sun and moon to kiss once more, and with their great gathering then they travel thunderingly North to begin their cycles again.

Town to town the news is sent by runner of the migration's location, and the People put on their yellow vestments, their yellow hats, their yellow sashes. The swarm will last a day, the air having the sound beaten out of it by Whu-ta-k'in wings, the incline of the atmosphere tipped by Whu-ta-k'in grace, the sun shied back by Whu-ta-k'in strength. To be in yellow is to be safe from the Whu-ta-k'in. But to be without yellow is to be a spot of reason in the Whu-ta-k'in's madness of hunger. There is not much to sustain the thinning beasts on the flight, and many fall exhausted off, decreasing the number so that the best and strongest of wing can survive.

For some of the People, there is an industry in finding those of the swarm that succumb to the journey, a salvaging of the holy bodies. Relics collected. Charms made. Spices extracted. Wings, if found whole, stretched out and mounted on filaments of whorl, a tool of reclaiming.

But the rest of the gathering searches out the food that will carry them to the next town, to the next thatch, to the next hillside. They will take livestock not protected by yellow; they will snap a stray dog; they would haul in one of the People if the People had not learned generations ago the miracle of yellow. Yellow.

The Whu-ta-k'in do not abide yellow. They see it. They sense it. They leave it be.

4.

"Be sure to put on your sash."

Wonjel's mother would remind her several times that day, and then herself fix the sash with a double knot. Wonjel had golden hair, aided by home-made dye, and a yellow sheath, and the sash was surely not needed. The more brazen of the People would not wear the sash. In their yellow tunics alone they would stand honored beneath the hurtling Whu-ta-k'in, chests pushed forward, faces upturned to look into the talons of the massive butterflies, or those who might be giant cousins of butterflies. Their courage would beam yellow into the souls of the migrating leviathans, soothing them, calming them, sending them peacefully away, sending them on to the quality of their business.

"Nika, now you have nothing to put away. Why do you love so to put away my playthings?"

Nika looked at Wonjel and cocked her head to one side, the way she did when she understood the meaning if not the message. "Place. Like place." She knew more, but could not say more. The words were matted thatch that stuck somewhere between the thinking and the making and lay dormant and exhausted in the heart and throat of the under-girl. She would hurl them if she could, just to see if they would bound or crawl, bounce or shatter.

Wonjel went over to her toy cabinet and took out a small wooden doll and two riding blocks, tossing them to the center of the floor. Nika clapped her hands and made a slight hop and ran over to pick up the first block, while eyeing with delight the second. Waddling on her powerful under-girl legs, she aimed for the cabinet and centered on it with all of her concentration. When she had put up the first block, she went for the doll. She had tricked the second block.

5.

Wonjel and Nika stood side by side between Wonjel's parents. Nika had maneuvered herself to be nearest Wonjel's mother, not Wonjel's father. They were not alone, and he was focused on the collection of the People, but Nika had summoned memory. Wonjel held Nika's hand, and Nika enjoyed the warmth of the hand, the feel of the skin - much smoother than hers - pressing itself into the recesses of her leathery palm.

"Now hold on tight. Nika can get spooked in a crowd. You do not want her wandering off too soon." Wonjel's mother was a maelstrom of unnecessary concerns, a temptation for forgetfulness. She would make rhymes for tasks, and sometimes the tasks would be changed to meet the need of the rhyme.

Wonjel adjusted her grip, but knew that Nika would go nowhere.

All along the town's center lawn, the People were standing, stretched on both sides, in family groups one or two deep. It was a small town. They had been told by the last town's runner from the night before that the swarm would be passing that day; that it had left the last inhabited place the day before and had rested the night on the open plain of Zigor: to rise that morning and pass through this hamlet of weavers and farmers and herders and hoarders of the word, before passing on, ever deeper South, their hunger growing, their anger needing ever more each day the yellow the People would provide.

Who knew what sanity to the soul of the Whu-ta-k'in the yellow brought? The People knew. How they knew it they knew not. Part of what becomes a people is the mystery that holds a people together. The People understood that the charm to hold the Whu-ta-k'in at bay, the key to making them a tool to be used and not a murderous bane to be hidden from, was the color yellow. Brilliant yellow. An unnatural color, product of combination, and elements mixed, that only those who might weave or paint could manage and rely on in quantity. The People learned it from the grandfathers who had learned it from their grandfathers who had learned it from a blinding, holy beginning; and there was no questioning it, especially as the swarm rose and could be, depending upon the act of the People, the beginning of things or the end of things.

And there they were! A shimmering cloud at first, but then a sense of undulation, and soon eddies of motion. The swarm seemed a living thing, not a collection of living things. It tilted on its axis and envisioned the vision of the town. It took measure and took stock and stuttered in its purpose long enough to consider its options. It spied the lawn and its borders of yellow, and - long accustomed to its promise - narrowed and began to focus on the wide strip of public welcome. As it closed, its life became the sum of its lives, and then the collection of lives, and soon each life alone, shored up with the next.

Across the green, one boy in yellow stepped out with his playmate in his tan tunic and walked with him hand in hand to the center of the lawn. He spoke a moment and pointed to the ground, obviously telling his playmate that here was his place, he would stand here. And then more children walked out, male and female, with under-male and under-female, boy and girl and under-boy and under-girl. When her mother tapped her sharply on the shoulder, a signal of time and not of command, Wonjel walked out with Nika still in hand; and when she reached the edge of the growing crowd she pressed Nika to the back of another under-girl, who looked around, but did not brace, her confusion and unwillingness to risk the punishment of disobedience stinging in her eyes like a housepest in a funnel trap. Nika reached out to grab this under-girl's post-like shoulder.

"Here. You stay here." And Wonjel was gone, a yellow blur back to her parents.

Her mother patted her again on the shoulder, pulled one strand of dried hair back into place. "Mom," Wonjel asked, looking up at the chin of her mother, "can I name my next Phe-butoo Nika?"

Wonjel's mother, who had returned her attention to scouring the edges of the swarm above, glanced down to her daughter as the swarm began to bend down towards the public green, and said, "Why, of course you can, dear. You can call it whatever you want."

Then the swarm banked sharply down, folding like a river folds when it is stumbling in declining gravity, and the Phe-butoo began to be taken up: sometimes in wholes, sometimes in halves, sometimes in pieces, the deep rumble of their screams hardly noticeable in the roar of so many wings so close together. The aerial ballet of the Whu-ta-k'in was breath taking, and in their yellow guards the People watched entranced and nearly crystalline as in intricate choreography the flock took in this season's indentured members of the Phe-butoo under-species, beginning the yellow-filled half of this year's ritual, wherein the playmates of a thriving community were exchanged.

6.

Nika did not so much like putting things back into place. But the comb was a marvelous machine. She could drag its bristles along her arm and have the most wondrous sensation. The tingles were a water that ran over her without the wet. And Wonjel laughed when she did it, which made her laugh too, and she sat naked on top of her tan tunic giggling and laughing and perhaps hearing all of what lept from Wonjel's lips, but not quite knowing where in her brain the patterns of Wonjel's sound should be housed; and so she let them go and laughed and laughed and laughed.

THE DOOR WITHOUT A KNOB

I noticed, first, that the stairs were just the right height. I could go up them at a good pace, down without jarring the knees. I thought there had been a few more actual steps to these stairs when I had originally auditioned the house - but, no matter, going up and coming down are now just right. I had not counted the steps originally, and impressions can get muddled with so much in a house to apprehend.

I did count the rooms. I have always wondered if you count the bathrooms and any pantry if there is a pantry, and even the kitchen, as rooms. Is a house of four rooms a bedroom, a bathroom, a kitchen and a den? Or is a four-room house three bedrooms, a living room, with one or two - or two and a half - baths implied, and the kitchen simply thrown in?

This house has eight or four rooms. Two baths, a kitchen, a storage room, two bedrooms, a living room, and the long laugh of a playful den.

As I thought about it, though, the storage room seemed larger. Really: what might you store in a room that large? I have no intention of stacking out of sight an entire boxed life; or giving away the floor space to shelves. There are closets and space under the bed to spirit the momentarily unused artifacts of life out of the way to wait in reserve.

So, at the last, five rooms it is. Or eight.

I had thought the whole place fully carpeted, but instead a rectangle by the front door four feet by eight turns practically into a fake tile runner: easier to clean, less likely to wear. I thought it had been carpet when I came in, but I could have been distracted by the brilliance of the windows: so many windows for the light to be happy with.

I am one to go through a door full force - neither angled, nor arm before body - so I am very pleased at the width of the interior room breaks. Most houses compromise. Some doorways are a squeeze; some a roundness of mouth, gasping for air. There is no need for any of that. A door is a way in and a way out, a welcome or a retreat. It does not need to call attention to itself. A door should be fulfilled through its use, not in its difficulty of navigation. Doors and doorways are means to locomotive ends. A homeowner should not have to ponder them.

I only just now noticed the window seats. I have fat cats that will claim them. In some homes the ledges are too high, but these seem lower than I have experienced elsewhere. My cats can conquer them without too great a series of exertions. And it seems the sun hits all of them, so a cat would not have to chase the light all day.

That half bath downstairs is just the perfect thing. I had thought at first it was a full bath, and I calculated: one more shower to clean. But it turns out that I was mistaken, and all the tubs are where they should be: in the baths upstairs, paired with the bedrooms they service.

I love the floor plan, the construction, the utility and the warmth of this house; but I am not sure that I can yet commit.

I have, now and again, ever since I arrived heard the wind in the eaves: ensnared, catching the wounded wanderlust of something - or perhaps the murmur of the central heating coming to the rescue of our air. At first, it was a coy moan, a whip of atmosphere hoping to find its rightful edges: a sound a man might respond to kindly, with nostalgia and the comfort of belonging. It seemed the sound of a first love dressing, or the hope of children sharing common secrets.

But as I reconsider the house, its cost and complexity, the sound has deepened, gotten itself wedged into something uneven and notched. Could be there is a gutter loose, or the fan in the HVAC needs a good calibration. There is almost stray desperation in the bravery of the ambient noise: a voice seeking repair. I do not know why I feel it so viscerally, as though it were speaking craft to my curious organs, singing poetry to the connection between my senses. It grows sad, an announcement of the need for regular upkeep, loneliness nailed on an exit.

There is much here to champion fondness. A house eager to please; a home where a family's imagination can run about in its underwear. I will keep it clearly in mind. But there are three others on the tour, and two came before. There is a practical magic to be worked before we can choose. Tell me, which was the door leading out, which way to the exit; and fathom, to you, does that still gathering melancholy sound, shrugging its shoulders woefully in the attic, seem ever so much like a gathering wail?

THE MAKING OF MERMAIDS

Standing at water's edge, ankle deep into the serpentine sea, I soon cannot feel the bleary pulse of my toes. I know it is still there, but the crisp of the water hides it deep within its own locket and I lose my specifics in its glimmer. The waves, of gentle period and gentle rise, are perniciously gentle today. Even with the water's crooning temperature, I can make it far enough out that coming back will not be a concern. I will be a spot on the waves a moment, arms and legs lazily windmilling the water, and then I will lapse recompensed beneath. I will transform.

Feet to fin, lungs to gills, skin to scale, commitment to capture.

It has been months since my husband was taken to sea by the mermaid. I do not think I will see him when I join the clan. By now, he has gone around the tip of our lands and to foreign coasts; or out into the deeper water where he can pride in the dark and slip caustically through the pressure made of the weight shouldered by an unattached ocean. His mermaid captor no doubt will be with him, a trail of unwanted oxygen, a sensuous fan of seaweed, an offer of crustacean delights.

Or he is drowned. And she has gone to another.

I do not think poorly of her. He would fish, suspended in the dull mechanism of his life, and tell me of what he had seen at only the edge of the eye, obscured as the sun dropped to drive the fishermen in. A presence; perhaps a protection. Later, he began to hear the song: the wail lifted barely at wave top, a rhythm that melded with his net, that melded with the oars, that melded at last with the unconscious patter of his salting heart.

He did not grow cold to me. I was his wife, the love he had when he was balanced, when he did not have to lean into ocean swell. I was four walls, the process of making his fish commercial, the everyday exasperation of respiration and unbroken gravity. I kept him while he was the automaton of his own upkeep.

But he had been raised a fisherman. The ocean would hold him. His catch was a gift of the sea. Into his existence there was placed the magical.

I was the practical end of his magical day. When I held the strength of his desires, there would always be the binary of the waves, the churning of the shallow. I would come up for air too often, and look to the dry as though it were a superior condition.

He believed in me less each day, and I could feel the hard edges of him growing briny.

When he finally saw the full license of her, he came to me to describe his opulent mermaid. Others believed, in silence; but he wanted to share, and he could only share his discovery with someone herself becoming a mythical woman. I was waxing, even then a commitment of the shadows. He talked of how at first there was but the back of her, driving the body down, racing below the waves and away from any man's sight. And then, once, there was the fluke. An emblem: the mark of claiming separateness. Soon the dive became slower. He stopped trying to call to attention the other fishermen, and instead luxuriated alone in the sight. And one day she dove no more, but propped herself in the water and gazed over the whole of the boat, over all the men engaged in dragging sustenance from the sea - but fixed on him: he at the back of the boat, his fingers stilled in their working the greedy magic of the nets.

He began to see her nearly every trip, and nights he would describe her to me, listing her boldness and her features and the baitfish moves she could expose, as his fingers drew incautious circles on the flat of my stomach, or looped unthinking in my hair. He moved his hands as though his fingers hid webbing. His lovemaking, always smelling just short of the shore, now reeked more of deep oceans, of the devilfish and the kraken: a thing of coiling and liquefaction and drifting as the antidote to drift. I could not fear his beak, but neither could I understand it. I was drawn in to where the monsters of the deep break human bone and join worlds together.

And then he was gone. The crew of the boat heard nothing, saw nothing, perceived no distress. There was no noticeable man-weight dragging in the net, tipping the boat; no army of arms and legs thrashing; no cry of imbalance. The sailors looked back to see him in his useful work, and he was gone. Where his feet should be already the water had erased his presence from the bottom of the boat.

Gone. No more. An absence at the back of the fishing craft; an emptiness in the process of needed work; something more for another to do. A clumsiness of air drawn crossly into lungs no longer. A history drawn to the end of its paragraph, with a seraph of oars and nets and fish heads. A story better in construction than in conclusion. A wife unhusbanded.

There is magic in this water. A calling. If I were to wade out until I could walk no further, then swim until I could swim no further, then sing into the waves until my singing were the sound of a net scraping stone, I could then perhaps become like my sister: a legend better in the telling than in the doing, a desire better in the sight than in the holding. I could lure men to my possibilities, their imaginations filled with completing what they do not have the rudder for; with knowing what they do not have the imaginations for; with wanting what they would no longer want upon breathing the understanding of it.

With practice and guile and the learning of my new school, I could bring, like netted market fish, working men to me. Any man who would be long with the sea. I could take them willingly down to their dear drowning, their embrace of the cold heart of water, their final kiss of nothing beyond their own reflected desires. I could leave ever growing legions of others like me unhusbanded: for a while their unapologetic hands would form the rounds of husbands, the explorations of men, the edges of being unfilled. They would learn slowly the terms of their abandonment.

I can make of many women sinful shells to be filled with the sea. I can be the agent of being no longer alone. Come with me. I breech and skim and dive and create whirlpools of emotion. Men fall in feral love with me for no other reason than I am imagined. Men fall in love with me for no purpose beyond proving they might have a special sight and a special need. I feel myself a history of the fluke, of the scale. Fill your emptiness with the craft of making. Come. Breathe the cleansing waters of longing. Be sisters.

UNTELLING PROGRESS

This time of year the streets are filled with the ventricular rush of Unicorn hunters. In their parties of ten or twelve they come lively back from two or three months of Unicorn hunting, the season dressed out and done, and their supplies and their wills exhausted; every bone-weary, crusted one of them ready to clothe themselves with the favors of civilization again; to have elated discourse with our less coarse citizenry, again. Each arrives ready for their privation-idealized dose of comfort and ease, but on their own terms.

As bold as though they owned all the elephant feathers in the treasury, they will blow into an establishment and order crowd sized portions of the best of everything. Keeping still warily sorted into their established hunting parties, they will space themselves in public areas with even geometries, the careful aggression of the season still at skin's surface and ready to touch solder into the cleft of any style of effrontery.

Ordinary citizens stay mostly out of their way, dancing at the periphery of their needs. We seek a slightly more edgeless portion of their wealth. Ragged hunters fresh from the Unicorn grounds are more than just a sight: they pay ungodly inflated prices for everything, and have a pit of requirements so deep there is an echo when you look into it. They have spent months in the wild seeking the greater fortune available through Unicorn tethering, and they reek of the effort, they reek of the desire for quantity over quality, of wanting it now, of now being all that there is in any mirror; and we will accept the burden of broken wares and rough civility for the imagination of cleaning up with towering profits afterwards.

These are not sportsmen to be trifled with. Mostly rich, mostly untamed, they come back from months without society, supplies that ran out early, the company only of a handful of the like minded, raw nerves even in agreement, a quickness to anger and a finality to conflict. These are the people inlanders secretly wish they were. These are the people the timid imitate when they are alone with their spouses, or drunk enough to imagine they can dominate the pathetically more sober.

Forgive me, but even beyond profit I look for their arrival.

One season, years ago, one hunter back from a particularly disjointed hunt along the ridge farthest out, and yet still considered to be Unicorn land, took a fancy to me. For three weeks I was her entertainment. My wife quickly packed what she could think of needing and migrated cross town to her mother's - and the Unicorn hunter and I extravagantly took over the house. I had to let the hired help run my business, and who knows what opportunities I lost during that time which is always normally filled with preternatural volume. But for those three weeks I hardly left our ungrounded bedroom; and, when I did get out, I was nowhere safe from her then-and-there immediate firebrand needs. I never got to the top of anything. We drank every ounce of Sorghum in the house, and twice I had to send out for more. Everything she did for the whole shackled time was an industrial process. For a week after she left, and the wife was cautiously back, we were finding lazily broken things, talking only of the physics of area, were restocking subtleties, trying to remember where the furniture had once been, and where we wanted it now.

The wife is still trying to become quick-pulsed attuned to all I learned in those three outlandish weeks. In places, she draws me back to our shopworn, habitual wants; in places, she takes the part of the gray area the ravenous Unicorn hunter left me, and tries to add it coyly to our mathematically inclined domestic rapture.

They can be wearying, but these Unicorn hunters give us so much. They separate themselves. They have a common list of attributes, a single-sized way of reacting, a single-sized way of being reacted to. You know what to expect, like it or not. You expect it. This a script you have seen before.

And, if you live on the edge of Unicorn country, you set your calendar by the hunt, adjust your trivial expectations, swap out the angels of your own character to match what you know is going to be needed to serve, profit, counterbalance, or simply reflect the disingenuous needs of massed Unicorn hunters.

Every year, a dozen Unicorn hunters lose their lives in the hunt. Falls, careless shots, feuds covered thinly as accidents, hunters who simply wander off and are never again seen. In the individual, no one much cares. In the collective, the statistics shriek out at you. Every year there is talk of whether we need the hunt or not. And when we say look at all the commerce this hunt supports, our uppity inlanders say who needs brothels, who needs bars, who needs Unicorn outfitters? They do not work out on plain paper how much of their own industry worms its way downstream to the backpacks of these hunters. They have no plan for what they would do with the girls now disemployed who would without Unicorn season become unemployed; no diagram for what people like me, with a small business squarely tuned around the comings and goings of Unicorn hunters, would do. No sense of the displacement, the expectations of ordinary lives that would, with prohibition, need to take a dizzyingly right turn.

And the cultural loss would be culturally devastating. Everyone knows of the Unicorn hunters. Everyone has his or her favorite Unicorn hunter homily. Everyone has an antonym for something he or she has seen placarded as true about Unicorn hunters. Myself, I have seen a Unicorn hunter shave her legs with a pocket knife: where would the imagination of all of my lackluster friends be if I did not have that truth to gut them with?

Of course, we have never seen a Unicorn strapped to the hood of a pick-up truck; or seen a Unicorn horn mounted on a baroque plaque leveled above some public bar. No one runs about in Unicorn chaps. I have not seen a Unicorn since .... Well, I have never seen a Unicorn. I suspect there are as many Unicorns in Unicorn country as there are waiting for the city bus where you live undisturbed and by weary train tracks. But that is not the point.

I have seen a whole town slapped silly by Unicorn hunters. I have seen men and women come out of months of unseen privation in the hunt and go split-handled wild with an energy that can come only from being soul deep into something so absurd it runs clockwork on its own.

These hunters are our left-handed interlopers at the convention of the right handed. They inspire us to wonders of waste and wrangling, they put the light back into our buttons. With one season they knock us off of our balance and give us our magical teeter again for the whole scarves-and-galoshes year.

And the wife said once she thought she saw a Unicorn. A white, shimmering thing, all muscle and lean, with hair that lay flat and orderly; with a huge silver spike jutting from the forehead, looking hand polished and as smooth as a stone kept too long in a fast running river. And she remembers thinking: that spike could hurt you.

THIS EXAMPLE

Every year I put on the chicken suit, come down to the plant, and parade all afternoon. The children of workers, the children of foremen, the children of managers, the children of office staff, the children of board members: all want to feel to find out if my feathers are real.

I walk in and out of offices around which, in my usual worker's coveralls, I would never be allowed. I rub the heads of people I have to stand aside for other days in the corporate section hallways.

I stare out through the beak, and have learned, through all the years I have been doing this, how to virtually ripple my coxcomb. My feet, more like bunny feet, I can shuffle and cock sideways and everyone laughs to see the chicken dance.

I don't get paid extra for this.

For days after I will be scratching the suit's starch from my skin, ironing with the flat of my hand the red welts that come up where the costume joints don't quite match my own. Once I had to call in sick after hours in the suit on an unseasonably hot summer day, and was nearly replaced right then as the company picnic chicken.

It is an honor, I'm told; but I think they size the employees up, select the one that looks less likely to damage the traditional suit, more likely to fit cautiously in with no severe stretch, no dithering of the fabric.

I haven't developed a good beer gut yet, so I slide easily into the aging company icon, and have done so for years. There are some tenured guys who tell me I am the best chicken of all; but I think they just want me to keep the job and prevent them from being asked to take it.

A boy of about three punches me flat in the thigh and I am glad for stiff over-weave, the quality backing.

One year the entire third shift got ball-eyed drunk, knowing hours would soon be cut and lay offs passed out, and tried to get a fire going in the sand pit drain to make for the largest chicken roast ever. That actually worried me. Beer and desperation don't make for clear thinking about the welfare of others. I ran about the yard, out of character, yelling at them to give it a rest, to go pick on some hot dogs and the chicken breasts laid out for that purpose. Once or twice they nearly had me and then a manager cracked open a bottle of cheap, under-the-seat bourbon, and the third shift lost interest in me.

I could have given up my acting career then, been satisfied as a line worker quartering chicken carcasses. No more giant chicken engagement once a year. No more giving children friendly nightmares, putting a comic face on the work we do.

But I persevered, and here I am one more year. By the end of this day I will be bone tired and bruised, sick of co-workers' families, bosses' families, and not so sick of that girl I've winged twice, barely contained in her halter top. But before I get two straggling volunteers to get me out of this awkward confabulation, I will wander out by the receiving dock and wait for the next truck load of chickens coming in to be processed: pressed against the wire of their cages, rattled from the road sickness of their cramped, long truck journey. Terrified, disoriented, crowded into silence except for the sudden movements of the truck — when their voices erupt, sounding like the squeak of their souls coming loose.

See. All is not lost. You have your champion.

THE REVENGE
OF THE HOUSE HURLERS

No one had suspected the depth of their emotion. As with any other class of professionals, we imagined they each had an affinity for their craft, some interest beyond a simple means to an income. We opined they had a guild, a professional magazine, poorly attended monthly meetings. Vividly ordinary. Half-respected, half-misunderstood, wholly unentertaining, all of them in possession of more details than those outside of the profession would ever care to know.

Not all that different from the brick-mites or the road benders or the fern illustrators or any denizens of the physically demanding lines of work.

We were unsuspicious. We kept our fingers comfortably collected and drew our solace from the cold well of ignorance.

But their sense of inadequate appreciation ballooned by the day, becoming grit in their teeth, a lost guttering stretch in the sinews. With the expert toss of each shed, the heave of each house, they resented more the shadows in which they labored, the public innocence of regard, the general unknowing void of the citizenry.

They would watch the televised annual bone-installers awards, wondering why there was no coverage of their awards; why the hurler of the greatest number of houses and sheds was not famous to school children, why the champion hurler could buy groceries anywhere unfounded by fame, appearing as ordinary as a fish on his bicycle.

From this side of the crisis, with the architecture of their grievances now discovered, no one blames them.

But we do suffer. Before the hurlers went on strike, every one of us would get a call every few months: a family we knew wanted us to understand they had been thrust into the air, water pipes bubbling loose in the exposed foundation below; masonry falling unthinking away; furniture striking out across the room; doors slamming open and shut; the divine feeling of passing with the house through the air in an arc of bittersweet satori; of seeing outlined within the window, before it shattered, the land passing beneath them; the shivering thrill of resettlement.

Yes, there was an occasional complaint, the odd injury or death; or a shed hurled or house hurled without its mate, and a matched pair thus being separated - but, for the most part, anyone engaged was electric at the wondrous event, happy to be hurled.

Yet, in the joy, it seems always the actual hurler was somehow forgotten. Why, yes, the hurling was stupendous - but what of the hurler? What of the hurler?

Anonymous and unknown, the hurler would shrug, sigh, open his notebook and find what address next was to be administered, and begin the long trudge to the new location, his huge, able hands nearly dragging the ground as he let those magnificent tools go slack and unwary.

We are a people who thrive on our hurling. Yes, there are other pursuits. But hurling has been part of our culture for as long as any of our civic jobs. If there are no house hurlers, then the dignity of lake tilters is diminished, light distenders suffer a loss of appetite for their manual labor. Tradespeople begin to suspect they are not valued, that the sum of their labor is the result of their action, not the application of their skill and their labor in their action.

And it is a loss of one more opportunity for our joy. There is no shaving the glee of someone whose house has been hurled.

But for now, the phone does not ring, with the caller unable to calm down, the house just having stopped its roll or slide, settling with a shiver and a shrug into its new place, workmen about connecting the utilities. There are no notices in the paper of new locations for houses, no offers for sheds seeking new pairings, houses seeking sheds. No one reminds lost visitors that a house has recently been hurled a mile north or south or east or west.

What to do?

There are a wealth of rumors, and the rumor-mongers go clack clack clack in their diligent and delightful work. But I think it will take some sort of appeasement, a show of our true gratitude. A public expression of our need for the house hurlers, an open and civic expression. Perhaps go to the monument massagers. Imagine, a stone house hurler at the center of town square, his mighty arm cocked, his eye in aim red and steel-sighted, springing at the waist and ready to hurl without prejudice or favoritism.

At the sight of it, maybe they would reconsider. Maybe they would forgive us.

ALSO BY KEN POYNER:

Sciences, Social, poetry
Constant Animals, mini-fictions
The Book of Robot, speculative poetry
Avenging Cartography, mini-fictions
Victims of a Failed Civics, speculative poetry